Alexander McCall Smith is the author of over eighty books on a wide array of subjects. For many years he was Professor of Medical Law at the University of Edinburgh and served on national and international bioethics bodies. Then in 1999 he achieved global recognition for his award-winning series The No. 1 Ladies' Detective Agency, and thereafter has devoted his time to the writing of fiction, including the 44 Scotland Street and Corduroy Mansions series. His books have been translated into forty-six languages. He lives in Edinburgh with his wife, Elizabeth, a doctor.

Praise for Alexander McCall Smith

'The fecundity of the McCall Smith imagination is one of the wonders of the planet. Von Igelfeld's adventures are truly, madly and deeply silly. Normally, McCall Smith's humour is almost entirely without cruelty. With von Igelfeld, however, he bends the rules . . . *Unusual Uses for Olive Oil* is his wildest, wackiest and funniest yet'

Scotsman

'McCall Smith has the gift of evoking an entire social atmosphere in very few and simple words'

Sunday Telegraph

'A treasure of a writer whose books deserve immediate devouring' Marcel Berlins, *Guardian*

'When it comes to the light touch, no one beats Alexander McCall Smith' James Naughtie, *Financial Times*

Unusual Uses for Olive Oil

ALEXANDER McCALL SMITH

Illustrations by Iain McIntosh

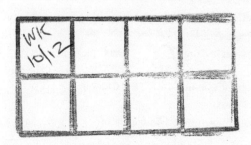

ABACUS

First published in Great Britain in 2011 by Little, Brown
This paperback edition published in 2012 by Abacus

A CIP catalogue record for this book
is available from the British Library.

ISBN 978-0-349-12010-2

Typeset in Galliard by Palimpsest Book Production Limited,
Falkirk, Stirlingshire
Printed and bound in Great Britain by Clays Ltd, St Ives plc

Papers used by Abacus are from well-managed forests
and other responsible sources.

MIX
Paper from
responsible sources
FSC
www.fsc.org
FSC® C104740

Abacus
An imprint of
Little, Brown Book Group
100 Victoria Embankment
London EC4Y 0DY

An Hachette UK Company
www.hachette.co.uk

www.littlebrown.co.uk

eins

The Award

Surprising? Astonishing? No, it was more than that, far more – it was shocking, quite nakedly *schrecklich*. Professor Dr Dr (*honoris causa*) (*mult.*) Moritz-Maria von Igelfeld, author of that definitive, twelve-hundred-page scholarly work, *Portuguese Irregular Verbs*, was cautious in his choice of words, but there were times when one really had no alternative but to resort to a strong term such as *shocking*. And this, he thought, was one such occasion. It was *ganz*, *erstaunlich* shocking.

The news in question was conveyed in the pages of a journal that normally did little to disturb anybody's equanimity. The editors of the sedate, indeed thoroughly fusty, dusty, crusty *Zeitschrift für Romanische Philologie*, a quarterly journal of linguistic affairs, would have been surprised to hear of any reader so much as raising an eyebrow over its contents. And certainly they would have been astonished to see one of their better-known readers, such as Professor von Igelfeld, sitting up in his chair and actually changing colour, reddening in his case, as he studied the small item tucked away in the news section of the review. It was not even the lead news item, but was at the bottom of the page, a mere paragraph, reporting on the announcement of the shortlist for a recently endowed academic prize. This prize, set up with funds left by a Munich industrialist of bookish tastes, was for the most distinguished work of scholarship – an article or a full-length monograph – on the subject of the heritage and structure of the Romance languages. What could possibly be controversial about that?

It was not the fact that the prize had been established that shocked von Igelfeld, rather it was the composition of the shortlist. There were three names there, all known to him, one very much so. As far as Professor J. G. K. L. Singh was concerned, von Igelfeld had no objection at all to his heading the list. Over the years he had had various dealings with Professor Singh, exchanging letters at regular intervals, and he had become quite fond of him. Certainly he did not agree with the rather unkind nickname that some scholars had given the celebrated Indian philologist

– the Great Bore of Chandigarh – indeed, von Igelfeld did not agree with nicknames at all, thinking them puerile and unhelpful. His own name, which meant *hedgehog-field* in German, had resulted in his sometimes being the butt of schoolboyish references, masquerading as humour, but of course he had always risen above such nonsense. It was true that Professor Singh was perhaps a little on the tedious side – indeed, he might well have been quite incontrovertibly so – but that was no excuse for calling him the Great Bore of Chandigarh. The British – ridiculous people! – and the Americans were the worst, he had noticed, when it came to this sort of thing, with the British being by a long chalk the more serious offenders. They saw humour where absolutely none existed, and it seemed to matter little how elevated they were – their jokes often being at the same time unintelligible and silly. Professor Thomas Simpson of Oxford, for example, a major figure in the study of vowel shifts, had referred to Professor Singh by this sobriquet and had remained silent in the face of von Igelfeld's protest that perhaps not everyone found Professor Singh boring. And he was no longer at Chandigarh anyway, von Igelfeld pointed out, which made the nickname out of date.

'He has been translated to Delhi,' von Igelfeld said. 'So the reference to Chandigarh is potentially misleading.

You must be careful not to mislead, Herr Professor Dr Simpson.'

This comment had been made in the coffee break at the annual World Philology Congress in Paris, and later that day, as the delegates were enjoying a glass of wine prior to the conference dinner, von Igelfeld had overheard Professor Simpson saying to a group of Australian delegates, 'I'm not sure if the Hedgehog gets it half the time.' He had moved away, and the flippant English professor had been quite unaware that his remark had been intercepted by its victim. A few minutes later, though, he found himself standing next to Professor Simpson at the board on which the table *placements* had been posted. Von Igelfeld was relieved to find that he was sitting nowhere near the condescending Oxonian, and he had turned to him with the remark, 'You will be happy, I think, to find that you are not sitting next to a hedgehog. They can be prickly (*prickelnd*), you know.'

It was a devastating shaft of wit, but it brought forth no response from its target, who appeared not to have heard. 'What did you say, von Igelfeld?' he asked.

Von Igelfeld hesitated. It was difficult to serve a dish of revenge twice within the same minute. 'I said that hedgehogs can be *prickelnd* if you sit next to them.'

Professor Simpson looked at him with amusement. 'I would never sit on a hedgehog if I were you,' he remarked airily. '...ery comfortable, as surely you, of all people, should know! But my dear chap, you must excuse me. I'm at the top table, you see, and I must get up there before the rank and file clutter the place up.'

If he rather welcomed the inclusion of Professor J. G. K. L. Singh's name on the list, he did not feel that way about the next name, which was that of Professor Antonio Capobianco of the University of Parma. He knew Capobianco slightly, and found his work slender and unconvincing. Two years ago the *Parmese* had written a book on the subjunctive in seventeenth-century Italian, a book that von Igelfeld had reviewed in polite but unambiguously dismissive terms in the *Zeitschrift*, almost, but not quite, describing it as *scholarly ephemera*. He would certainly not have chosen Capobianco had he been a judge, but at the same time he could understand that there might have been political reasons for including him on the list. It was nice to put Italians on lists – they so appreciated it; Italians, von Igelfeld was convinced, had a profound need to be loved by others and consequently were always reassured to see their names appear on any list. He had even heard that they tended to get upset if they were left off negative lists – such as those that ranked the most corrupt countries in the world. 'But we *lead the world* in corruption,' one Italian prime minister had been said to complain. 'How can they put us below *Mali*?' So there could be little doubt but that Capobianco would be very pleased to see himself on this shortlist and would presumably make every effort to bribe the judges to decide in his favour – or, if he did not, some of his friends and relatives could be expected to do so on his behalf. But he would never win.

But then there was the third name, and that was where enthusiasm and mild irritation were succeeded by outrage. Professor Dr Dr Detlev-Amadeus Unterholzer, the journal announced, had been nominated on the basis of his work on Portuguese verbs – work which enjoyed a considerable reputation not only in Germany but throughout the world. *His research has put Regensburg's Institute of Romance Philology on the map*, the journal concluded, *and deservedly so. This makes him a very strong candidate for the award of this prize.*

It was difficult to know where to begin. Unterholzer had been von Igelfeld's colleague for a considerable time. Their relationship was not a simple one, as there had been a number of issues over the years – none of them von Igelfeld's fault, of course – because of which the friendship between them, if one could call it that, had been strained. Most notably there had been the incident of Unterholzer's dog, the unfortunate dachshund, Walter, or Dr Walter Unterholzer, as the

8

Librarian, Herr Huber, had so wittily called him. This dog had lost three of his legs in circumstances for which Unterholzer blamed von Igelfeld, and the poor animal was now obliged to get about on a prosthetic appliance involving three small wheels. Walter had, some years previously, disgraced himself by coming across and eating a small collection of bones. These bones had not been intended for consumption by dogs, rather they were sacred relics of particular interest to the Coptic church, being the bones – or some of them – of the late Bishop of Myra, none other than St Nicholas. Thereafter, Walter had become an object of veneration within the Coptic church as he had consumed holy relics and was therefore, in a sense, a reliquary, even if an ambulant one. He had enjoyed a brief period of veneration in a church, occupying a small gilded kennel before which pilgrims would kneel. Unfortunately, many pilgrims expressed surprise at the barking sounds which emerged from this kennel–reliquary, and so in the end Walter was restored to his original owners, the Unterholzers.

Von Igelfeld's responsibility for Walter's unfortunate injury had led to ill-feeling, but even putting that *casus belli* aside, there had also been numerous occasions on which Unterholzer had sought to obtain some advantage over von Igelfeld. Some of these were minor – and could be forgiven – but others were of such a serious nature as to remain a stumbling block in the way of normal relations. One thing was clear, though – that von Igelfeld was the better scholar. Unterholzer had written his own book on Portuguese subjunctives years ago, a minor insubstantial book, which had concentrated only on a few modal verbs. Certainly that work was not fit to be mentioned in the same breath as *Portuguese Irregular Verbs*, and indeed never was, at least by von Igelfeld, who always made sure that he left a gap, a silence, between any uttering of the names of his own book and Unterholzer's.

It was the glaring disparity between their respective contributions to Romance philology that made this announcement so hurtful. If anybody's work had put Regensburg on the map, it was his, von Igelfeld's, that had done so. A few people abroad might have heard of Unterholzer, von Igelfeld conceded, but they would not necessarily know him for his *work*. They might have seen him at conferences, perhaps, where they surely would have noticed, and perhaps even discussed, Unterholzer's rather vulgar nose; not the nose of a scholar, thought von Igelfeld. Or they might have come across a reference to Unterholzer's book while looking for something more substantial, such as *Portuguese Irregular Verbs* itself. But they would certainly not have bothered to sit down and read Unterholzer's observations on modal verbs.

10

So why, then, had Unterholzer been shortlisted for what was, after all, a rather generous prize of fifty thousand euros? As von Igelfeld was thinking of this outrage, he was joined in the coffee room by the Institute's librarian, Herr Huber.

'Anything interesting in the *Zeitschrift*?' asked the Librarian. 'I haven't read the latest issue yet. It's on my desk, of course, but I've been terribly busy over the last few days, what with my aunt not being quite as well as she might be, poor soul.'

The Librarian lost no opportunity to mention his aunt, a resident of a nursing home on the outer fringes of the city. This aunt, who enjoyed bad health, was the subject of long monologues by the Librarian, who laboured under the impression that his work colleagues were interested in endless details of her complaints and afflictions.

'No, she has not been all that well,' mused the Librarian, quite forgetting the question he had just put to von Igelfeld. 'She has blood pressure, you know. I did tell you that, didn't I? Yes, I think I must have. She's had it for a long time.'

'Everybody has blood pressure, Herr Huber,' said von Igelfeld cuttingly. 'If one did not, then one's blood would simply stay where it was, rather than going round the body. Your aunt would not last long without blood pressure, I can assure you. Nor would you, for that matter.'

11

This last remark was an aside, but even as he uttered it, von Igelfeld wondered whether the Librarian had, in fact, much blood pressure. There were some people who gave the impression of having a great deal of blood coursing through their veins – robust and ruddy people who moved decisively and energetically. Then there were those who were pallid, and slow in their movements; people through whose veins the blood must move sluggishly, at best, with only the pressure expected of a half-inflated bicycle tyre. The Librarian belonged in that group, von Igelfeld thought.

Herr Huber laughed. 'Oh, I know that. I meant to say that she has the wrong sort of blood pressure. It's either too high, or too low. I can't remember which. And there is one sort of pill for high blood pressure and another for low. You have to be terribly careful, you know. If you took the pill for high blood pressure and your blood pressure was really too low, then I'm not sure what would happen. Heaven forfend that anything like that should happen to my aunt, of course!'

'Indeed,' said von Igelfeld. 'That would be a most unfortunate occurrence.'

'Of course, these days pills are made in different colours and shapes,' the Librarian went on. 'One of the nurses said that most pills used to be white, which could lead to bad mistakes in their administration. Now

12

they are different colours and have markings on them.' He paused to take a sip of his coffee. 'She – my aunt, that is – used to have a large red pill that she had to take before she was settled for the night. Sometimes I was there when they gave it to her. She called it "my red pill" and I once asked her, "What is that pill for, Aunt?" and she said, "I am not sure. It is my red pill and I have been taking it for a long time. Perhaps it is meant to turn me red."'

Von Igelfeld stared glassy-eyed at the Librarian. 'And did she turn red, Herr Huber?'

The Librarian laughed. 'No, that's the funny thing. She took that red pill for years, always saying that it was intended to turn her red, and I thought she was just joking. Then when I said to the doctor, "I see that you have prescribed a pill to turn my aunt red!" he answered, "That's right."'

Von Igelfeld said nothing.

'And the funny thing,' continued the Librarian, 'was that the red pill was for anaemia. It was iron, you see. And if she had not taken it, she would have appeared very pale. So the pill really was intended to turn her red.'

Von Igelfeld pursed his lips. 'Your aunt's affairs are of great interest, Herr Huber,' he said. 'But will you forgive me if I return to the question you asked me when you came in? You asked me whether there was anything of interest in the *Zeitschrift*. I would like to answer that question now, if I may.'

The Librarian took a sip of his coffee. 'Of course you may, Herr Igelfeld.'

'Von Igelfeld.'

The Librarian inclined his head. 'Yes, of course. Do you know there is a doctor who attends at my aunt's nursing home who *added* a von to his name? Suddenly it was there and he was most insistent on its use. He would very pointedly correct people who omitted it.'

Von Igelfeld sighed. 'If he was entitled to it, then it should have been used. But I would prefer not to discuss matters of etiquette, if you don't mind, Herr Huber. You asked me if there was anything of interest in the *Zeitschrift*. And I would like to answer that question.'

'But you must,' said the Librarian. 'You know, I don't think that one should leave questions hanging in the air. Have you noticed how politicians do that? Somebody asks them a question and it sits there unanswered. I don't approve of that at all, do you, Herr von Igelfeld?'

Von Igelfeld began to feel the back of his neck becoming warmer, as it often did when he talked to the Librarian. Sometimes it felt as if he were in one of those dreams where he had to get somewhere or

14

perform some task and it was just impossible to do it. Talking to the Librarian was a bit like that, and in an ideal world he would not have had to talk to him at all. But there were often occasions when the Librarian was the only other person in the coffee room and one could hardly sit there in complete silence.

'About the *Zeitschrift*,' said von Igelfeld. 'There is a mention of the Institute. Perhaps you would care to see it.'

He passed the journal over to the Librarian, pointing to the offending item at the bottom of the page. Herr Huber took it from him and, adjusting his glasses, began to read.

When he had finished, he looked up at von Igelfeld and beamed with pleasure. 'Well, this is most remarkable news, Herr von Igelfeld. It's very good to see the Institute get recognition. And how gratifying it must be for our dear colleague, Herr Unterholzer, to get a prize. Fifty thousand euros! That is a very substantial prize, even if our currency is worth next to nothing these days because of bad behaviour by everybody except Germany. My aunt says that certain countries should—'

Von Igelfeld's eyes narrowed. 'You do not need to remind me of the elementary facts of economics, Herr Huber. But thank you, anyway. Returning to the matter in hand, it is, as you say, a very good thing to see the

Institute get publicity. But do you not find it surprising that they should seek to give Herr Unterholzer, of all people, a prize?'

The Librarian looked puzzled. 'Not really,' he answered. 'Herr Unterholzer is an established scholar. I'm sure that he richly deserves recognition for that book of his. Not that I have read it personally.'

Von Igelfeld suppressed a smile. 'Not many have,' he said. 'It is not a very widely read book at all. In fact, I would venture to suggest that nobody at all reads it nowadays.'

The Librarian shrugged. 'I wouldn't know. There's a small library in my aunt's nursing home, but I don't think it's there. And I don't think my aunt would be interested in Herr Unterholzer's book – not at her advanced age.' He paused. 'But you do not seem very pleased, Herr von Igelfeld. Why is this?' He peered at von Igelfeld over the top of his glasses. There were times when the Librarian saw nothing, but there were times when he saw everything. 'I would have thought that the triumph of one would be a triumph for all. Would you not agree?'

'Of course,' said von Igelfeld, hastily. 'It's just that in this case . . . well, I think that there may perhaps be a mistake, Herr Huber. I would love Professor Dr Unterholzer to win some sort of award. But at the

16

same time I would always want the award in question to be – how shall I put it? – fully merited.'

The Librarian looked blank, and von Igelfeld continued with his explanation. 'You see, it would hardly be very satisfactory if he, being a person who undoubtedly deserves at least some recognition, were to be given a prize that perhaps he does not actually deserve, if you see what I mean.'

The Librarian did not. 'Do you mean that they might be mixing him up with another Professor Unterholzer?' he asked. 'Some Unterholzer . . .' He waved a hand in a generally northerly direction. 'Some Unterholzer up in Hamburg or somewhere like that? Is that what you're suggesting?'

Von Igelfeld shook his head. The Librarian was either trying to appear obtuse or was simply not picking up the very clear point he was making. He would have to spell it out, and he now did so, leaning forward and lowering his voice even though they were still the only ones in the coffee room. 'Herr Huber, has it occurred to you that they have mistaken Unterholzer for *me*?' He pointed a finger to the text in the *Zeitschrift*. 'They refer, as you have seen, to the putting of Regensburg on the map. Well, who did that? Professor Unterholzer? Or did *I* do it? With *my* book?'

The Librarian was a fair man, and faced with so direct a question there was only one answer he could give. He did not in any way want to diminish any glory that might be coming Unterholzer's way, but he had to admit that of the two works of scholarship, von Igelfeld's *Portuguese Irregular Verbs* was undoubtedly the more significant. 'That is quite possible,' he said. 'But it's a great pity if it is true.'

'Indeed it is a pity,' said von Igelfeld, sitting back in satisfaction that his point had been agreed to. 'There are many regrettable mistakes made in this life and some of them are not only a pity but are painful – to all concerned. I refer, of course, to the decision made by Athens to send its fleet to Syracuse during the Peloponnesian War.'

The Librarian nodded. 'That was most regrettable. The victory of Sparta was not a good thing, in my view.'

Von Igelfeld tapped the table in emphasis. 'Indeed it was not. But mistakes are made, and this is possibly one. Not perhaps of quite the same magnitude as the mistake made by the Athenians, but a mistake none the less.'

The Librarian looked thoughtful. He could not recall making any mistakes himself, but others certainly did. 'You know something, Herr von Igelfeld,' he began. 'I heard of the most extraordinary mistake that was made a few years ago. Please forgive me if I've already told you about it, but there was a lady in my aunt's

18

nursing home whose first name was Inge. That, in itself, is unexceptional enough, but as it happens there were two Inges in the home. One is now no longer with us, I regret to say, but the other is. She has the room two doors down from my aunt's old room – before they moved her to the new wing, that is. That wing took an awfully long time to build, you know. The builder went bankrupt. He was Polish, I believe, and although they can be very good builders they can sometimes get into a bit of a financial mess.

'This lady by the name of Inge received a letter one day. But before I take this any further I should tell you that her surname was Schmidt and the other Inge, the one who did not live in the old wing but had a room under the clock tower – or the place where the clock tower used to be before they knocked it down and built a storeroom – that Inge's surname was Schultz. She was Frau Inge Schultz, and my aunt told me – discreetly, of course – that she had the most terrible habit of moving the top set of her false teeth while you talked to her. The teeth came out over her lower lip and you saw the artificial pink gums. It was a nervous habit, really. She didn't intend to cause offence.

'Anyway, this letter that Frau Inge Schmidt received was in reality addressed to Frau Inge Schultz! The handwriting was indistinct, you see, and the young man who sorted the mail misread it. Easily done, I suppose, but it meant that Frau Inge Schmidt received a letter addressed to Frau Inge Schultz, and started to read it. Of course it began with the greeting *Dear Inge* and so she assumed it was for her. But the letter went on about all sorts of things that meant nothing to her, and was signed at the end by a name she just did not recognise. Klaus, I think it was. Or possibly Karl. I must ask my aunt about it when I go to see her this evening. She remembers these things. But let us work on the assumption that it was Klaus.

'Well, she reached the end of the letter and, being a very polite person, decided that she would just have to write back to this Klaus person and tell him some of the things that were happening in the nursing home. So she did, and a few weeks later she got a letter addressed back to her. She had put her room number on her letter of reply and so the young man in the post room had delivered it to her although this time the writing was clear enough. He didn't look at the name, you see – he just looked at the room number.

'So it carried on for some months. She continued to get letters from Klaus and he got letters from her. Then he wrote and announced that he was coming to visit her because he had to be in Regensburg for some reason or other. He turned up and asked for room fifty-two – or whatever it was – and they directed him to it. Then he realised that he had been corresponding for some time with a complete stranger.'

The Librarian paused, allowing the full impact of the story to sink in.

'And so?' said von Igelfeld.

'They became very good friends. He decided that he rather preferred this Inge to the other one and they continue to write to one another to this day. He sends her books and magazines, and she has knitted a whole set of very attractive bathroom accessory covers for him. My aunt showed me a picture of one of these – it was very beautifully worked, I must say.'

Von Igelfeld rose to his feet. 'I must dash, Herr Huber,' he said. 'As usual, it has been a great pleasure talking to you.'

'We could continue later, over lunch if you wish, Herr von Igelfeld,' said the Librarian, also rising to his feet. 'That is, if you are free.'

'I am not,' said von Igelfeld. There were limits to the comity one had to show colleagues, and these had been reached, indeed had been exceeded, even before the conversation had come to an end. Besides, he had letters to write. The mistake that he had uncovered could not be left unchallenged. If there had been confusion, then it would have to be dispelled, painful though that duty might prove to be.

*   *   *

He travelled to Berlin by train, enduring a journey that could have been pleasant had it not been for the annoying conversation of his fellow travellers, some of whom insisted on talking on the telephone at great length about matters of a most personal nature. Von Igelfeld's stares of disapproval were met with a blank response from a woman who spent at least fifteen minutes describing an operation for ingrowing toenails and the difficulties she had had with her insurance company over the resulting claim. Why should they pay such a claim, von Igelfeld asked himself. It was nobody's fault that her toenails had grown in; or, if there were fault, then surely it would be her own, for not cutting them correctly in the first place. That was the trouble these days; nobody was prepared to accept responsibility for anything, not even for the state of their toenails.

By the time the train drew into the Hauptbahnhof von Igelfeld felt in a thoroughly bad mood. Berlin, however, lifted his spirits, with its wide skies, its architecture and its air of being at the centre of something. This was undoubtedly a place where power was exercised and decisions were taken, even if some of these decisions, as in the case of Unterholzer's nomination, were unfortunate ones. Well, if Berlin was a physical metaphor for decisions, then it was also a metaphor for the confrontation and rectifying of past mistakes and wrongs. There had been the horrors and moral disaster of the thirties, followed by the pain and penitence of the forties and fifties. These had been followed by the monstrous mistake of the Wall, and again that had been rectified by that structure's dismantling. Wrongs, rectification, renewal: a mantra we might all commit to memory, he thought.

The offices of the Leonhardt Stiftung, the body in charge of the prize, were not far from the main campus of the Freie Universität. Von Igelfeld was familiar with the university, as he had recently given a seminar at the Languages of Emotion Centre, or Cluster of Excellence as it was now called. That was not a very modest way of describing oneself, he had thought at the time. One might be excellent – indeed his institute in Regensburg was undoubtedly excellent – or largely excellent, if one left Unterholzer out of the equation – but that did not mean to say that they should change their name from the Institute of Romance Philology to the Cluster of Excellence of Romance Philology. How ridiculous people had become, he thought, in their scrabbling after recognition and the funds that came with it. He had written *Portuguese Irregular Verbs* without so much as a penny of public money, although its publication undoubtedly made him a cluster of excellence in these new, ridiculous terms. And who would head a cluster of excellence? Did a cluster have a director, or did it have a pole, rather like a magnetic pole? Hah! It would surprise them if he went into the Cluster of Excellence nearby and asked for the pole. Of course the director might be a real Pole, and that would cause confusion. How funny!

He was well received at the Leonhardt Stiftung, where he was shown into the waiting room outside the director's office.

'Herr Unterholzer will be with you in a moment,' said the secretary, flashing a smile in his direction. 'He is just completing an important telephone call and asks that you would be good enough to wait.'

Von Igelfeld froze, halfway into the sitting position, poised immediately above his chair. He wondered whether he had heard correctly. Had she said *Herr Unterholzer* or had he heard *Herr Unterholzer* because Unterholzer had been on his mind? He knew that the mind played tricks on one, especially if one were tired after a long journey. It was not unusual to hear, or read, things that were not really there but were suggested to us by the subconscious. Professor Freud had written something about that, he thought, although it was difficult to remember exactly where Professor Freud had written anything.

'Did you say Herr Unterholzer?' he asked.

'Please do continue to sit down,' said the secretary. 'Yes, Herr Unterholzer is the director of the Stiftung.'

For a few absurd moments von Igelfeld imagined that he had stumbled upon the most extraordinary piece of chicanery. Unterholzer had relatively few commitments in the Institute and could easily spend three days a week in Berlin without anybody's being any the wiser. It was perfectly possible, then, that he was moonlighting as the director of the Leonhardt Stiftung while still holding down his position in Regensburg. That sort of thing was common in Italy, of course, where there were people known as pluralists, who had jobs in more than one university. Thus a professor in Parma might also be a professor in Bologna, or even Rome. He had heard of one man who was a professor in Bari while at the same time being a professor in Trento – cities separated by an immense length of Italian railway track. This professor, drawing a full salary from both institutions, had taken to conducting some of his seminars in Milan, expecting students to travel from each city to meet him there. That was all very unsatisfactory and would not be tolerated in Germany, thought von Igelfeld. Nor would the German authorities tolerate another Italian situation he had heard of involving a university in a city where neither the professors nor the students lived, thus making the institution a virtual shell. Shells, however, can get grants from the European Union, which had a long history of giving grants for non-existent tomato crops in places like Sicily and Greece.

If Unterholzer was the director of this foundation, then he was showing the most remarkable brass neck in putting himself on the shortlist for the prize. Von Igelfeld considered that not only was this unprincipled, it was probably also criminal, and for a few delicious moments he imagined Unterholzer being arrested in the coffee room at the Institute and dragged off while the Librarian went on about somebody's having been arrested in his aunt's nursing home for stealing from the kitchens or something of that nature. What a thought! *Unterholzer disgraced over self-awarded prize*, the headlines would read. And the report would continue by saying, *His colleague, Professor Dr Dr Moritz-Maria von Igelfeld, author of* Portuguese Irregular Verbs, *remarked sadly yesterday that nobody had been aware of Professor Dr Unterholzer's double life. 'Criminals can be very cunning,' the professor said* . . .

The door at the end of the waiting room opened and a rather rotund man peered out. He was smartly dressed in a double-breasted grey suit and was sporting a carnation in his buttonhole. The man smiled at von Igelfeld. 'My dear Herr von Igelfeld,' he said, stepping forward to shake his visitor's hand. 'What a pleasure it is to see you. And how kind of you to call in during what must be a very busy visit to Berlin. That, you see, is the trouble with Berlin. All our visitors are so very busy we have to fight for the tiniest part of their time.' And here he indicated a very small amount of time by placing a thumb and forefinger very close to one another.

So, thought von Igelfeld, this is another Unterholzer altogether; Unterholzer is not holding down two positions, and yet this is an Unterholzer, as the name on the door so proudly proclaims. He must therefore be some relative of Unterholzer – and that would explain why Unterholzer was shortlisted for the prize. And just as fraud was being excluded, something as corrosive was in the process of being uncovered – gross and blatant nepotism.

As he sat down in the chair on the other side of the director's desk, von Igelfeld glanced quickly at his host's nose. Unterholzer's entirely unsuitable nose was very individual, and it would be interesting to see whether this Unterholzer's nose was in any respects similar. If it were, that fact would provide an additional element of proof in his case. Even if the director denied any relationship to Detlev Amadeus Unterholzer, then the evidence of genetics, incarnate in a large, potato-farmer's nose, would clinch the matter.

He looked at the nose. Yes, it was large, and yes, there was the same sort of uneven bumpiness that was so prominent a feature of the topology of Unterholzer's nose, the ur-nose, so to speak. If only the director would turn slightly to the left, von Igelfeld thought, then I would be able to see whether there is that very characteristic bulge on the bridge.

The director cleared his throat. At the same time, he shifted slightly in his seat and his left hand went up to his nose, as if to check that there was nothing wrong. Von Igelfeld looked away guiltily.

'It is a very fine day,' said the director nervously. 'Sometimes Berlin can get very hot, you know. You have those mountains to keep you cool. Here we are at the mercy of the hot winds of the plains.'

'Indeed,' said von Igelfeld. 'I have always been fortunate on my visits to Berlin. I have always found the weather very agreeable.'

The director nodded, acknowledging the compliment. 'We do our best, of course.'

There was a brief silence. Then the director spoke again. 'I wonder if there is any way in which the Stiftung can help you, Herr von Igelfeld? We are familiar with your institute, of course, and we are certainly anxious to engage further in the cutting edge of language research. We have a major programme at the moment in neuro-linguistics.'

'I am not interested in that,' said von Igelfeld cursorily. 'These days they are adding neuro- to everything.

Neuro-ethics, neuro-theology and so on. It will be neuro-tennis next, I imagine.'

The director laughed. 'That would be neuro-tic,' he said.

Von Igelfeld stared at him. 'I beg your pardon?'

'Nothing,' said the director, waving a hand in the air. 'All I would say is that in addition to our neuro-linguistics programme we have funds to support more conventional fields. We have people working on the acquisition of pidgin languages, for example. And we also have a very interesting research programme down in Frankfurt looking into the ability of animals to under-stand language commands. Most dogs respond to the *sit* command – that is more or less universal. It's clear that domestic animals acquire a small vocabulary – a passive knowledge of language, of course – but what is not so clear is whether there are some languages that are easier for dogs to acquire than others. Is it purely a question of how many syllables there are, or are there other factors involved? How do animals cope with tonal languages, for example? All in all, it's a fascinating bit of research.'

Von Igelfeld nodded. 'Yes, it must be. But I must point out that I have not come with a view to discussing a grant. I have come about the prize you have announced.'

The director raised an eyebrow. 'I'm afraid that we

are somewhat past the closing date on that one,' he said. 'The judges – of which I have the honour to be one – have recently announced their decision on the shortlist. Perhaps you haven't seen it. There are three names, actually, and one happens to be . . .'

'Your cousin,' interjected von Igelfeld.

The effect of these words was instant. The director's jaw dropped, and he moved back in his chair, as if pushed by an unseen hand. 'You do not imagine . . .' His voice was wavering and he did not finish the sentence.

'I assumed that you and Professor Dr Unterholzer were cousins,' said von Igelfeld. 'There is, after all, a certain family resemblance.'

'In what way?' stuttered the director.

'In the . . .' Von Igelfeld was about to say *in the nose*, but stopped himself. This meeting was not going well.

The director had now recovered his composure and leaned forward in his chair. 'I must assure you, Herr von Igelfeld, that we are not related in any way. He is Unterholzer and I am Unterholzer too. But it is a very common name, you know. I can understand how if you are called von Igelfeld you may assume that all other von Igelfelds are relatives, but you are fortunate in that respect. We Unterholzers do not make the same assumption.'

Von Igelfeld was beginning to feel embarrassed. His moral outrage had been replaced by the realisation that he had been wrong after all. And he regretted barging in with his accusation; it must be bad enough to be called Unterholzer in the first place without then being accused, groundlessly, of nepotism to other Unterholzers. 'I am very sorry, Herr Direktor,' he said. 'I have spoken out of turn. I assumed – quite wrongly – that you were some relative of our Professor Dr Unterholzer just because of the name and your no— and other factors. Please forgive me.'

The director smiled indulgently. 'There is nothing to forgive, Herr von Igelfeld. It would make no difference if I were related to this Unterholzer of yours. I would never let such a factor sway me in any decision.' He paused. 'I take it that this is what you came to see me about? You were concerned about the possibility that ill-informed people might think that the presence of the name Unterholzer on that list was indicative of some sort of improper favouritism? Well, I suppose there is nothing that one can do to stop base-minded people thinking that. But it does not make it true, does it?'

'Not at all,' said von Igelfeld. 'But that was not really the aspect of the prize that concerned me. I came to see you because I thought that the committee had perhaps made a mistake and confused one person for another.'

The director raised an eyebrow. 'In what way?' he asked. 'In what way can we have been mistaken?'

Von Igelfeld did not find it easy. 'It occurred to others – not necessarily to me, of course – but to others that when the committee wished to honour Romance Philology in Regensburg, then they might have been thinking of my own work, *Portuguese Irregular Verbs*, rather than Professor Unterholzer's somewhat less well-known work. That is what some people thought, and they brought their doubts to me. I, of course, dismissed these concerns, but thought it politic to raise the issue with you. That is all.'

The director sat quite still. 'You say you are the author of *Portuguese Irregular Verbs*, and not Professor Unterholzer?'

Von Igelfeld caught his breath. There had been a mistake after all. 'I am,' he said. 'It is my work that you are talking of.'

The director put a hand to his brow. 'Oh dear,' he said. 'This really is most unfortunate. The committee received reports on a number of meritorious works. For some reason, the members were under the impression that *Portuguese Irregular Verbs*, which I must say is very highly regarded, was the work of Professor Unterholzer. That is why he was shortlisted.'

I knew it, thought von Igelfeld. I was right all along.

There has been a terrible mistake. Then he thought: fifty thousand euros.

'However,' said the director, 'as it happens no damage has been done. The judges met again yesterday and reached their final decision. The prize has been awarded to Professor Capobianco. So it really makes no difference. Had it been awarded to Professor Unterholzer, then it would have been very complicated. But the jury has come up with its verdict and the matter has gone the other way. We have yet to announce the outcome, of course.'

Von Igelfeld bit his lip. 'You mean that the judges decided that Professor Capobianco's book was more worthy than *Portuguese Irregular Verbs*? Is that what you're suggesting? That they preferred *ephemera*?'

The director winced. 'I wouldn't have put it that way,' he said. 'Not in the presence of the author of *Portuguese Irregular Verbs*, your good self. But I suppose that is an inevitable inference from the outcome.'

The two men stared at each other for a few moments. Von Igelfeld found his eyes drawn to the director's nose. It is the same nose, he said to himself. It is definitely the same nose. And that is just too much of a coincidence to be discounted. There was something not quite right about this situation, but he could not put his finger on it. It seemed very unlikely that the members of the prize committee could have laboured under the mistaken view that Unterholzer had written *Portuguese Irregular Verbs* unless . . . unless they had been deliberately misled by the director of the Stiftung, who no doubt had been charged with the duty of preparing a précis of each nominee's achievements. If this Unterholzer were a nepotistically inclined cousin, as von Igelfeld now once again suspected, it would not have been difficult for him to effect such a deception.

Von Igelfeld rose to his feet and took his leave of the director. There would be plenty of time to think about this matter on the train back to Regensburg; back to Regensburg and away from scheming, duplicitous Berlin, full, as it was, of Unterholzers and their equivalent. And during this time of reflection he could ponder his next move. He could confront Unterholzer, revealing that he knew that this was a case of an Unterholzer awarding a favour to another Unterholzer; or he could remain silent, rising above the whole sordid matter. He decided on the latter. There was, after all, an element of doubt, no matter how suspicious it all looked. And a man was innocent until proved guilty in a court of law, and that presumption should be extended to Unterholzer, even if he did not deserve it.

So when von Igelfeld saw Unterholzer in the coffee room at the Institute the next day, he congratulated him warmly on being shortlisted.

'I have heard that I have not won it,' said Unterholzer. 'And I did tell them, you know, that if anybody should be on the list it should be you. I told them that *Portuguese Irregular Verbs* was the book that really put this place on the map.'

'You did?'

'Of course.'

There was no doubt that Unterholzer was telling the truth, decided von Igelfeld, as he looked down into his cup of coffee. How complex this world is, he thought; how easily may things appear to be one thing and then prove to be another. And how easy it was to see the worst in humanity when what we should really be looking for is the best.

'That was very kind of Professor Dr Unterholzer,' said the Librarian. 'Do you not think so, Herr von Igelfeld?'

zwei

An Intriguing Meeting

It was only a few days after von Igelfeld's return from Berlin that the issue of marriage was raised in the Institute's coffee room. At the end of the discussion nobody was quite sure who had been first to mention the matter; it might have been Professor Dr Dr Florianus Prinzel, or it might have been Unterholzer – von Igelfeld was later unable to recall exactly who had started the debate. He did know, however, that it was not the Librarian, Herr Huber, whose wandering conversation was entirely reactive, and never introduced a new or challenging topic.

And marriage was a challenging topic as far as von Igelfeld was concerned. As a young man, still a student, he had had the occasional girlfriend, but these relationships had never got anywhere very much, as the young women in question rapidly tired of von Igelfeld's single-minded devotion to scholarship, his tendency to divert any conversation to linguistics, and his utter lack of any sense of romance. *You're a very nice boy, Moritz-Maria,* one of these girlfriends had written in her parting letter, *but do you really think that girls are interested in hearing about Portuguese verbs, or whatever it is you spend all your time thinking about? If you do, then for your own sake I must tell you that you really don't understand how we think. Sorry to be so frank, but you really need to know: Portuguese verbs are* not romantic!

Von Igelfeld had been puzzled by this letter. He did not mind the rejection so much – his feelings towards the writer of the letter had been barely lukewarm – but he wondered why she should at one and the same time be terminating the relationship as well as describing him as very nice. If she liked him, then why was she ending things? And how could she speak for all girls and say that they were not interested in philology? How did she know that? Then, finally, there was the terrible howler at the end: *Portuguese verbs are not romantic.* That was terribly funny, unintentionally, of course. Portuguese was a Romance language, everybody knew, which meant if there was one thing that Portuguese verbs were, it was romantic! Silly girl!

Much later, it had occurred to him that marriage

would be a desirable state, and he had decided to make an effort to get to know better his dentist, the charming and attractive Dr Lisbetta von Brautheim. To this end he had presented her with a copy of *Portuguese Irregular Verbs*, which he subsequently discovered she was using to stand on while operating her dental drill, as the bulky book was just the right height in relation to her supine patients. His feelings might have been hurt by this, had not a far greater cause for offence soon presented itself. This arose after he had recommended her to Unterholzer, who needed to see a dentist about a worrisome crown. The encounter had been both professionally and socially productive, as Unterholzer later revealed that he had seen Dr von Brautheim for lunch. It was by then hardly appropriate for von Igelfeld to renew his own invitation for lunch, for Unterholzer had proposed and, *mirabile dictu*, been accepted.

Von Igelfeld tried to put a brave face on this disappointment, but it was hard. With both Florianus Prinzel and Detlev Amadeus Unterholzer married, he was the only one of the three professors of the Institute who was single. Herr Huber, of course, had never been married and von Igelfeld considered it inconceivable that anybody would ever wish to marry him, but the Librarian was a special case, and was not really counted for most Institute purposes. The difficulty for von Igelfeld was that marriage, it seemed to him, was an impossibly

41

complicated matter. If it were a simple process – on a par with, say, obtaining a passport or answering a call to a university chair – then he would have felt quite up to it. But there was the whole business of asking somebody to marry one, and how on earth was that done? *Will you marry me*, although an unambiguous enough question, none the less seemed rather abrupt and could always elicit the simple answer *no*, which would be devastating. And when exactly did one make the proposal? He had read that this could be done over dinner, but it was not specified at what stage of the dinner it was appropriate to pop the question. Did one have to do it before coffee, or was it better to get round to the subject at the coffee stage of the meal? What if the restaurant were noisy, as so many restaurants were, and the question was not heard at all?

But most daunting of all was the task of meeting somebody suitable. Von Igelfeld's life, revolving as it did around the Institute and its affairs, rarely brought him into contact with suitable, unmarried women. It was true that some of the women staff were single, but they tended to be rather younger than von Igelfeld and he was realistic enough to understand that these young women would hardly be attracted by a man in his late forties, even if he prided himself on carrying no extra flesh and being attractively tall. He had heard that women liked tall men, and in that respect at least he

42

would be a good catch, but height alone would never carry the day with these young secretaries, with all their giggling and their fascination with the glittery world of popular magazines. And of course they had very little in common in terms of intellectual interests, of which, he believed, they had none at all.

He briefly considered Herr Huber's assistant, a woman in her early thirties, whom he believed to be unmarried. But when he got to know her better, through her occasional appearances in the coffee room, he realised that some of the Librarian's worst traits had rubbed off on her and he did not think that he could tolerate for any length of time her rambling conversation on matters of very little interest. For the rest, there were few opportunities. There was the odd social occasion, including, now and then, dinner parties, but everybody at these functions appeared to be married or to have other existing arrangements. It sometimes seemed to von Igelfeld that he, alone, was alone.

The conversation about marriage – whoever started it – got on to the topic of the advantages of cooking for two.

'It's much cheaper,' said Prinzel. 'Indeed, we usually cater for six, and then freeze the remaining four portions for use at a later date. It is called an economy of scale, I believe.'

'How very interesting,' said Herr Huber. 'The chef

at the nursing home – the one my aunt is in – was telling me that he has to cater for forty-two and—'

'Yes, yes, Herr Huber,' said Unterholzer. 'The real point is that there is no difference – in labour terms – between making one portion or two. They both take exactly the same time. Another argument in favour of the married state!'

Unterholzer threw von Igelfeld a glance at this stage, which von Igelfeld returned icily.

'How interesting,' said von Igelfeld. 'At the same time, one must not forget that cooking for two reduces one's culinary choices by exactly fifty per cent.'

There was a silence while this remark was digested. Prinzel looked particularly puzzled. 'Why?' he asked. 'I really don't see . . .'

'Nor do I,' snapped Unterholzer.

Von Igelfeld smiled. 'A moment's thought will confirm the truth of what I've said. Any two people will naturally like different things. If, therefore, there are, shall we say, twenty available recipes, we may assume that person A will like ten and person B will like ten. These preferences will be different, because people have different tastes. So there will probably only be ten that will be accepted by both people. Some of these will not be the first choice of both. Each person will therefore probably only get five courses that he really likes. That restricts choice by fifty per cent.'

44

There was a further silence, eventually broken by the Librarian. 'My aunt cannot abide spinach. If she has spinach—'

He did not finish. 'I don't see that at all,' interjected Unterholzer.

'Oh, I assure you, Herr Unterholzer, she has never been able to eat—'

Unterholzer ignored the Librarian and addressed von Igelfeld again. 'A single person would like ten of the twenty, you say? Well then, if he is sharing with somebody else they're surely going to find ten that they both like, or can eat. So in each case he's having ten. That's not less choice – it's the same.'

Von Igelfeld smiled. Unterholzer was just not getting the point. Prinzel, who was also puzzled, now steered the conversation back to marriage. 'There are many shared moments in a marriage,' he said. 'That is one thing you discover when you marry.'

'But, forgive me, Herr Prinzel,' said von Igelfeld. 'Forgive me for pointing out that surely most people would know that *before* they get married. Spending time together, I would have thought, is a fundamental feature of marriage – something that everybody knows.'

'There is knowledge and knowledge,' interjected Unterholzer. 'You may think that you know something and then you discover that you didn't really know it – not in the full sense. So . . .' and here he glanced at von Igelfeld, 'so unmarried people – those whom nobody has ever wanted to marry . . .' and he looked at von Igelfeld again, 'those people, with all due respect to them, may be ignorant of some of the more subtle implications of the married state. That is my view, for what it is worth.'

Von Igelfeld bit his lip. It was quite intolerable to have to sit and be condescended to by Unterholzer, of all people. He knew that he should have maintained a dignified silence, but he just could not let this pass. 'Many unmarried people are unmarried by choice,' he said. 'They are often rather more discerning people: people who are not afraid of their own company. Not always, of course – but often.'

'I'm not sure about that, Herr von Igelfeld,' Unterholzer replied. He was about to continue, but the Librarian had something to add.

'My aunt never married,' he said.

It had been a very unsatisfactory conversation from von Igelfeld's point of view. He could discount anything that the Librarian said, of course, as Herr Huber had very little knowledge of the world. He knew something about book classification and paper conservation, perhaps, and he appeared to have some arcane – and entirely useless – knowledge of the ins and outs of nursing homes, but when it came to any other topic, including marriage, he was not to be taken at all seriously. Unterholzer could also be ignored most of the time, even if it was important to listen to what he had to say if only to refute it. He was married, of course, but von Igelfeld was very doubtful as to whether his colleague had learned very much from that experience. So he, too, could be safely discounted. But then it came to Prinzel, and here was a fish of an entirely different stripe. Von Igelfeld admired Prinzel, and had done so since their student days, when he had accorded to Prinzel that devotion that the scholar-poet classically gives the hero-athlete. Prinzel knew about women, who had flocked to him even in their student days, and if anybody were going to influence von Igelfeld's view of marriage, it would be Prinzel.

It was significant, then, that Prinzel should have sauntered into von Igelfeld's office later that day and taken up the theme of the coffee room conversation. 'Interesting remarks were made this morning,' he said, as he walked over to gaze out of von Igelfeld's window. He often did this, and von Igelfeld tolerated it. Unterholzer, by contrast, was never allowed to look out of that window and was always sharply censured if he did so. 'I do not mind your admiring my view, Herr Unterholzer,' von Igelfeld had said. 'But I would prefer you to ask permission before you do so. It is only common courtesy, I believe.'

Unterholzer had snorted. 'I did not think that a view is a private thing, Professor von Igelfeld,' he had said. 'Perhaps you will feel the need to correct me, but I must point out that the trees and hills at which I am looking do not belong to you. And if they do not belong to you, then I fail to see why I should ask your permission to contemplate them.' He threw a challenging glance at von Igelfeld, before adding, 'Or perhaps I'm missing something?'

Von Igelfeld had been unable to answer this, and had been obliged to get up from his desk and draw the blind, so that Unterholzer could not continue to look at the view uninvited. 'Forgive me, Herr Unterholzer,' he said. 'But I find the sunlight a little bit fierce, and, as I'm sure you will agree, it is disconcerting to be blinded by light *when one is trying to get on with one's work.*'

Prinzel, of course, needed no such direct reprimands. He could look at the view as much as he liked, as far as von Igelfeld was concerned. Indeed, he would happily provide him with a chair at the window so that he could enjoy the view in comfort, if that proved to be necessary.

'Yes,' mused Prinzel. 'There is no doubt but that marriage is a fascinating subject.' He paused. 'Don't you agree?'

'Of course,' said von Igelfeld. 'I am aware of that.

48

I am proposing to read a bit more about it. I believe that Montaigne has something to say on it.'

Prinzel raised an eyebrow. 'Montaigne was the sort who would have something to say on . . . the physical side of marriage. But that is not the issue. The real issue is the pleasure that marriage brings in the domestic sense. I cannot tell you how comfortable it is not to have to iron one's shirts.'

Von Igelfeld glanced at Prinzel's shirt, which was beautifully neat and smooth, with razor-like creases down the sleeves. Then he looked down at his own shirt, which was so badly looked after by his Polish housekeeper, who was becoming distinctly slipshod in her attention to his clothes.

'You would perhaps benefit from that sort of attention,' said Prinzel.

'Perhaps,' said von Igelfeld.

'And then there are the delights of the table,' went on Prinzel. 'Did I tell you what I had for dinner last night? No? Coquilles St Jacques, followed by a very fine piece of Swiss beef. How about that?'

Von Igelfeld looked up at the ceiling. He had enjoyed a heated-up can of soup and a cellophane-wrapped sandwich that he had bought from a small shop round the corner. 'Very tasty, no doubt,' he said. 'Of course, there is a restaurant nearby that does that sort of thing. I sometimes go there.'

'But imagine having it in your own home,' said Prinzel. 'It always tastes so much better than in a restaurant. And restaurants are always full of rather lonely people, I find. It's often very melancholy.'

Von Igelfeld said nothing. Prinzel did not intend to offend, but it was clear that von Igelfeld was one of these lonely people who could be encountered in restaurants. He was not lonely, of course; he had the *Zeitschrift* to keep him company and there were always new articles to read, but it was also undeniably true that when he went to restaurants he usually sat by himself. In fact, he always sat by himself, apart from one occasion when somebody had been put at his table because of a lack of a place elsewhere. That had been an interesting experience, with von Igelfeld snatching the opportunity to glance at his fellow diner from time to time and speculating mentally as to where he came from and what he did. He was a respectable-looking man with a pleasant, prosperous air to him, and von Igelfeld would have rather enjoyed a conversation with him – had they been introduced to one another, which they had not.

He looked at Prinzel; he would have to allay his friend's concerns. 'I am quite satisfied with my domestic arrangements, Herr Prinzel,' he began. 'You will have observed, I think, that I am not wasting away. I do not think, therefore, that you need concern yourself about whether I am getting enough to eat. But thank you, none the less, for your interest in this matter.'

Prinzel continued to look out of the window. 'Yes, Herr von Igelfeld, that is clear. You are not in imminent danger of starvation. Nobody is suggesting that. However . . .' He paused, turning round to face von Igelfeld. 'However, it is true, is it not, that you are not exactly overweight. In fact, you are thin. And it is also true that your clothes . . .'

Von Igelfeld waited for Prinzel to continue. Prinzel, in his view, was in no position to criticise his clothes. He himself liked wearing a completely unsuitable fawn-coloured waistcoat that von Igelfeld had long wanted to discuss with him. Perhaps this would be his opportunity.

'Yes, my clothes, Herr Prinzel? I am interested to hear about my clothes. It is always useful to get the advice of one whose own sartorial expertise is so clearly of such a high standard. Your waistcoat, for instance—'

He did not have the chance to finish. 'There is nothing wrong with your clothes,' Prinzel continued hurriedly. 'When other people attack them, I never hesitate to defend your wardrobe.'

Von Igelfeld's eyes narrowed. Why, he wondered, should others attack his clothes? It was not a comfortable discovery to make – to find out that there were people, unnamed people, who were in the habit of singling out one's clothes for adverse comment.

'Who are these people?' he asked.

Prinzel waved a hand towards the window, as if to take in the entire population of central and eastern Bavaria. 'Oh, there are many of them. People of no consequence, no doubt. I cannot list them all at present; they are too numerous.' He looked at von Igelfeld almost apologetically. 'But it is not your clothes that I wish to discuss. That would be very rude. Nobody likes to hear their clothes described as fit only for a second-hand shop or for distribution to the less fortunate members of society. Nobody likes that sort of comment, do they? No, it is not your clothes I wish to talk about, it is rather a very direct question which my wife asked me to raise.'

Von Igelfeld waited. He liked Ophelia Prinzel. He liked Prinzel, too, and it was only for this reason that he was putting up with this increasingly trying personal conversation. Had it been Unterholzer raising such issues, the outcome would certainly have been quite different. The niceties would have been observed, of course – they always were – but Unterholzer would have been left in no doubt at all about the inappropriateness of what was being said.

'This question, Herr Prinzel: I am most interested

to hear it. Has it anything to do, I wonder, with the work of the Institute?'

Prinzel shook his head. 'Oh, no, it has nothing to do with that.'

'Well then?'

Prinzel looked embarrassed. 'It is not a question that I would normally ask of anybody. In my view, such matters are strictly private. But you know how women are.'

Von Igelfeld nodded, which surprised Prinzel. He does not know that, he thought. He knows nothing about that subject, poor Moritz-Maria.

'Of course you do,' said Prinzel. 'Well, my wife, Frau Prinzel—'

'I am well aware of her name,' interjected von Igelfeld. 'I would not expect your wife to be called Frau Unterholzer, would I?'

They both smiled at the joke, which went some way towards dissipating the tension that had grown up through this conversation.

'Of course not,' said Prinzel. 'It would be very strange if I went round saying to people, "This is my wife, Frau Unterholzer." That would be very strange indeed!'

Von Igelfeld laughed. It was a very good joke, and he felt proud of having made it in the first place. Prinzel had a good sense of humour, he thought, but rarely managed to originate a comment as amusing as this.

'Or indeed if I introduced her as Frau von Igelfeld!' continued Prinzel.

Von Igelfeld's smile faded. 'But there is no Frau von Igelfeld,' he said. 'I do not think, therefore, it would be at all amusing to make such a ridiculous mistake.'

Prinzel agreed. 'No, you are right. I was merely thinking of another example of the same thing.'

'An impossible example,' said von Igelfeld.

Prinzel nodded. 'Quite.' He drew himself up. He was every bit as tall as von Igelfeld and his bearing was still almost as impressive as it had been when they were students in Heidelberg and he had cut a dashing figure in the Korps. 'Quite,' he repeated. 'Now, this question that my wife suggested I should ask. It is quite a simple question, but please, do not feel under any compulsion to answer it. You are perfectly free to claim what our American cousins call the Fifth Amendment and to say nothing.'

'I have no cousins in America,' said von Igelfeld. 'Do you, Herr Prinzel?'

Prinzel shook his head. 'Not as far as I am aware. It is a figure of speech.'

'And a very misleading one,' snapped von Igelfeld. 'It could cause considerable confusion if people thought that there were all these cousins in America, when in reality there are not.'

'Of course; of course. But this question . . . What my

wife wished to know is whether she could possibly introduce you to a lady of her acquaintance. That is what she wanted to know.'

Von Igelfeld frowned. 'Why?' he asked.

Prinzel looked at his friend. He was not making it easy. 'This lady has only recently come to Regensburg,' he explained. 'She is from Stuttgart, I believe, and she does not know many people here in Regensburg.'

'Then why did she come?' asked von Igelfeld. 'If you are from Stuttgart, where you know many people, is it wise to come to Regensburg, where you know nobody?'

'She was left a house here,' said Prinzel. 'Her cousin was a bachelor and she is his heir. He was the Graf Hauptdorf. Hauptdorf und Praxis, to give him his full title.'

Von Igelfeld sat quite still. He had seen the Graf's obituary in the newspapers, and had been reminded of a visit he had paid to the house itself, which was often open to the public. 'The Schloss Dunkelberg? He left that to her?'

Prinzel nodded. 'It is a very fine house, as you know. And so she thought that it would be best to leave Stuttgart and come over here to look after the place. It has extensive grounds, as you are no doubt aware.'

'They are very fine,' said von Igelfeld. 'And the house

itself is of more than mere passing architectural interest.' He paused. 'How did Frau Prinzel meet this lady?'

'They found themselves seated next to one another at a bridge class,' said Prinzel. 'It is a class for complete beginners that my wife has joined.'

Von Igelfeld nodded. 'Bridge is a very suitable game for ladies,' he said. 'One would not want one's wife to be taking up some more dangerous sport – such as motor-racing, Herr Prinzel.'

'There is no danger of that,' said Prinzel. 'My wife cannot drive, you see.'

'Then she is unlikely to take up motor-racing,' agreed von Igelfeld. 'But to return to this lady – I would be perfectly happy to meet her, if Frau Prinzel would care to arrange an introduction. I will be able to show her round Regensburg, perhaps.'

'That is precisely what my wife thought you might do,' said Prinzel.

Von Igelfeld hesitated. 'And her husband too, if he would care to come.'

Prinzel shook his head. 'But there is no husband, Herr von Igelfeld. This unfortunate lady lost her husband at least ten years ago, I'm told. He was an industrialist. Herr Benz. The late Herr Friedrich-Martin Benz.'

'Oh yes?' said von Igelfeld. 'And what did this Herr Benz make?'

'I have no idea,' said Prinzel.

'They are very energetic people, these industrialists. They are always making something. I have never heard of the late Herr Benz, but no doubt he made many things.'

Prinzel laughed. 'He must have been very busy.'

The conversation concluded at that. Prinzel said that they would give von Igelfeld several dates for a possible dinner and he could choose one that fitted with his social commitments. Von Igelfeld thought about this for a moment: he had no social commitments, as far as he knew, but it would not do to make Prinzel aware of that. 'I'm sure that we shall find a suitable date,' he said. 'We might have to wait a few weeks, but we shall certainly find one.'

'Good,' said Prinzel. 'And my wife will no doubt make us all a very tasty meal. Do you know, by the way, what we are having tonight? Venison stew. I have always liked venison, Herr von Igelfeld. Do you like it?'

Von Igelfeld shrugged. He could not remember when he had last eaten venison. It had tasted good, though; he was sure of that. 'Who doesn't? But I find that one doesn't want too much of it.'

'Of course not.'

Prinzel returned to his own office, leaving von Igelfeld to his thoughts. The Schloss Dunkelberg? Interesting. He had gone there with a small group from the local historical society and he had seen that it had a very interesting library. He had thought at the time: the people who own this place obviously never open any of these books – what a waste! Well, what if a place like the Schloss Dunkelberg were to come into the hands of somebody who really appreciated a library of that size and magnificence: what then?

Nothing more was said of the matter over the next few days, and it might have resulted in nothing had it been left to Prinzel and von Igelfeld themselves. But Ophelia Prinzel, once enthused, was not one to lose interest in something quite as entertaining as match-making. She had grave doubts as to the suitability of von Igelfeld for anybody, but she was aware that sheer demographic reality meant that there were many women, particularly those, like Frau Benz, in their late forties, who would never find a husband unless they were prepared to scrape the bottom of the barrel. As a result of this, many otherwise unmarriageable men came under scrutiny by women who would be none too fussy in their assessments. She had a close friend who had, in fact, recently settled for a man who had lost several limbs and an ear in a series of accidents. 'He is admittedly not complete,' the friend had said. 'But when there are so few men available, what choice do we women have? Half a man is surely better than no man at all, would you not say?' Although this argument might at first have appeared less than compelling, sober reflection revealed it to be a good one, and such reflection, Ophelia felt, might also boost the case for Moritz-Maria von Igelfeld. Granted that he was an impossibly dusty scholar; granted that he was completely set in his ways; granted that he had not the slightest idea of how women thought and behaved; in spite of all of that, he was none the less a man, and a tall and rather distinguished-looking one into the bargain. With a little attention to his clothing, he might pass muster as a very suitable escort for an outing to the opera or a trip on the Rhine. And the rest, surely, could be worked upon; for von Igelfeld could be considered a *project*, in the same way as one considered an old house or a dilapidated vintage car as a project.

As for Frau Benz, Ophelia thought that there was very little wrong with her. She was a fairly large woman, it had to be admitted, but this gave her an undoubted presence. She was clearly generous, too, as she had on more than one occasion met Ophelia for coffee and cakes in the Café Florian and insisted on paying the bill.

'Herr Benz left me very comfortably provided for,' she said. 'Dear man! He remarked once, "My own memory may fade when I am no longer here, but I shall do all I can to ensure that the memory of my money lingers on." Coffee and cakes are well within the budget!'

She had frequently spoken of her late husband, and his interests. 'He was a very active man,' she said. 'He loved gardening, riding, flying, carpentry, painting . . . There were few things Herr Benz could not do.'

'How useful,' said Ophelia. 'Such men are few and far between.'

'Indeed. Do you know, we never needed to employ a workman to fix anything. My husband would roll up his sleeves and tackle any task that arose. He would not rest until whatever it was that needed to be fixed was fixed.'

'There must have been many women,' mused Ophelia, 'who would have loved to marry Herr Benz. You were very fortunate.'

This compliment was acknowledged with gratitude. 'You would have liked Herr Benz, Frau Professor Prinzel. And I fear that I shall never find another man who is his equal.'

'If one turned up, though,' said Ophelia, 'I take it that you would be pleased?'

Frau Benz thought for a moment. Then she smiled coyly. 'Such a man could be a delightful companion.'

This exchange, and a number of others like it, planted the idea in Ophelia Prinzel's head that were she to come across a suitable man, she should try to introduce that man to Frau Benz. And why not? There is a natural tendency on the part of those who are happily married to assume that those who are not should be similarly placed. And yet this tendency is usually confronted with a marked dearth of available men. In this case, a mental inventory of single men known to the Prinzels resulted in only two names: Herr Huber, the Librarian at the Institute, and Professor Dr Dr von Igelfeld. Herr Huber was impossible, of course, and could be completely ruled out in any circumstances, for any woman, no matter how desperate, and so attention shifted to von Igelfeld, who was also largely impossible, but perhaps not quite so much a lost cause as the unfortunate Herr Huber.

The arrangement of the introduction proved easier than she had imagined. It transpired that neither von Igelfeld nor Frau Benz was occupied on a particular Friday evening two weeks hence. An invitation to dinner was extended, and accepted. Frau Benz, of course, was not told what the purpose of the evening was. 'We are giving a very small dinner party,' said Ophelia. 'Our table, alas, is not large. There will be only two guests.'

'A large table is no guarantee of a pleasant evening,' said Frau Benz. 'The most charming dinner parties I have been to have been very small affairs. *Intime* is best, I think.'

Von Igelfeld was aware of the purpose of the evening, and felt a certain excitement in the prospect of meeting the new owner of the Schloss Dunkelberg. There was a large illustrated history of the house published by a local publisher, and he obtained a copy and made a point of reading it before the evening took place. It was a very badly written history, in his view, with a very small number of footnotes, but at least it would give him plenty to talk about with Frau Benz and he would be able to keep up with her should she mention – as he thought she well might – the extensions that were built in the late eighteenth century.

He also took great care in the choosing of his clothes for the evening. Ophelia Prinzel had said that it would not be formal, but this did not mean, of course, that all formality would be thrown to the winds. Von Igelfeld was aware that there were those who did not wear a tie to dinner, having been shocked to see a picture in the newspaper of an important dinner in Berlin at which the male guests – or a considerable number of them – did not appear to be wearing ties. He had referred to this in the coffee room one morning and had been further shocked by the response of his colleagues.

'Lots of people don't wear ties any more,' said Unterholzer. 'It is thought to be more comfortable not to. And why not? Why should people make themselves uncomfortable?'

Von Igelfeld had looked at him with icy disdain. 'And shirts?' he said. 'Are they to be abandoned too? We would undoubtedly be more comfortable without having to bother with things like sleeves and collars, would we not?'

It was an unanswerable objection, a devastating point, but Unterholzer had seemed unmoved. 'That may be the way we're going,' he said. 'Perhaps we shall eventually see through the need for clothing altogether – other than in the winter, of course. But in summer we can all be children of nature again.'

The conversation had ended there. Von Igelfeld did not feel it wise to encourage Unterholzer in these anarchic, unsettling sentiments, lest his colleague be tempted to start divesting himself of his baggy and badly cut shirt there and then. Children of nature indeed!

And now, standing before his wardrobe, he reached inside and took out his best blue-fleck suit, a suit that he had bought in Cologne fifteen years previously and used only very occasionally – for major family gatherings, such as the seventy-fifth birthday of his uncle, when the entire extant von Igelfeld family – all forty-three members of it, including the Austrian branch – had gathered in Munich for a celebration. The suit had been expensive, made from Scottish tweed, and beautifully tailored. It would be just right, he considered, for an evening such as this; Frau Benz, as the proprietrix of the Schloss Dunkelberg, would undoubtedly appreciate good cloth, and would realise that . . . well – and he blushed at having to think in these terms – she would realise that he was from the same *circle* as she was. That was delicately put, he thought. The landed gentry, to whom she belonged thanks to the inheritance of the Schloss Dunkelberg, did not like crude terms such as *class* – he blushed further; they made the easy assumption that people were either *possible* or *impossible*. It was not a judgement based on anything one could put one's finger on, and it certainly had nothing to do with wealth. A poor man – a man without so much as a bean – could be perfectly possible, while a man of substance might be completely impossible. It was impossible to say how possibility – and impossibility – came about. Impossible. But von Igelfeld was in no doubt that he could not possibly be considered impossible.

He dressed with care and made his way to the Prinzels' house, arriving at the front door at exactly the time stipulated by Ophelia in her invitation. He knew there were people who arrived for dinner five or ten minutes late, claiming that this was not only fashionable but also considerate towards one's host or hostess, however von Igelfeld did not subscribe to that view. If people wanted one to arrive at seven thirty-five, he thought, then they would invite one to do so. If they wanted you to arrive at seven thirty, then they would invite you for seven thirty. And the same applied to railways, he reflected. If the railway authorities wanted their trains to leave five minutes late, then they would specify that in the timetable. But they did not.

Prinzel welcomed him at the front door. 'You're early,' he said.

Von Igelfeld pointedly looked at his watch. 'I don't believe I am,' he said. 'My watch is very accurate, and it says seven thirty precisely. And that I believe is the time for which your wife invited me.'

'Oh, well,' said Prinzel. 'You're not early, then – you're prompt. Like Immanuel Kant. He used to go for his walks in Königsberg at the same time each day and the people of the town used to set their watches by him.'

'That was very good,' said von Igelfeld. 'Things appear to have deteriorated since then. I imagine that there are very few philosophers today who keep regular hours.'

Ophelia appeared in the hall. 'You're early, Moritz-Maria,' she exclaimed.

Von Igelfeld bowed politely. 'I am not,' he said. 'But if you would prefer it, I can go away and then return again. Some other day perhaps.'

'No, please don't do that,' said Prinzel. 'Come into the salon while Ophelia finishes with her preparations. Our other guest is yet to arrive. I expect she'll be here in about ten minutes or so.'

'About then,' said Ophelia. 'That would be normal.'

Prinzel led the way through a corridor to the salon. In this corridor, opposite a coat rack, was a long, ebony-framed mirror, hung on the wall. It was positioned in such a way as to allow one to adjust one's clothing before setting out, and von Igelfeld could not resist giving his blue-fleck Scottish suit an admiring glance as he walked past. He froze. Out of the corner of his eye, he noticed that the back of his jacket had a hole in it, and through this hole could be seen not only the shirt he was wearing but also the braces that he was using to keep his trousers up. And worse than that – a quick, discreet movement to the jacket revealed that the seat of the trousers was similarly afflicted. Moths, he thought.

'Everything all right?' asked Prinzel from the end of the corridor.

Von Igelfeld dragged himself away from the mirror and walked briskly down to where his host was standing. 'Perfectly all right,' he said, adding, to cover his dismay, 'I must say, Herr Prinzel, that you have made a very fine home of this house.'

Prinzel beamed with pleasure. 'Ophelia has a very good eye for decoration,' he said. 'She tells me that when she was a little girl she used to spend many hours decorating and redecorating a large doll's house that she had. Perhaps her ability stems from those days.'

Von Igelfeld nodded. He was thinking of what he could possibly do to deal with the embarrassing holes that he had discovered. He wondered if he should simply confide in his hosts and ask Ophelia whether she had needle and thread to pull the gaping fabric together. But if he did that, he would have to remove his trousers and hand them over to her to carry out the emergency repairs. And what if Frau Benz arrived and discovered that the other guest had already removed his trousers? She would wonder, surely, what sort of dinner party she had been invited to and, as a respectable widow, would surely leave immediately; unless, of course, Ophelia drew her aside and explained to her the real reason for the removal of the trousers. But then she would think, no doubt, that it was very odd that a guest should come to a dinner party in such a state in the first place. She moved in circles, no doubt, where people did not have holes in their clothes, at least not in Germany; British gentry, of course, regarded it as entirely appropriate and indeed a mark of distinction to have shabby clothing, but then the British were very notably odd about this and most other matters.

'You'll have an aperitif, Herr von Igelfeld?' Prinzel asked. 'A vermouth perhaps? Or should I offer you a choice between French or German wine? Both are available.'

'Then I shall have German,' said von Igelfeld. 'Rhenish, if you have it. The French need no encouragement.'

'Indeed not,' agreed Prinzel. 'There are many people who need no encouragement, and the French are certainly among them.'

Prinzel left the room to fetch the glasses, leaving his guest alone. Looking about him, von Igelfeld searched the room for a possible solution to the problem of the holes in his clothes. He could not expect to find a needle and thread – not in a salon – and anyway, if he did, he had no idea how to use them. Perhaps there would be some sort of paper clip that would do the trick; there was a writing bureau in one corner of the room and that would be an obvious place for such a thing. Moving quickly, he crossed the room, opened the top drawer of the bureau, and rifled through the contents. There were envelopes, letters, a stick of sealing wax – the typical paraphernalia of a writing bureau drawer. There were no paper clips.

'Are you looking for anything in particular, Herr von Igelfeld?'

Von Igelfeld froze. Then slowly he turned round to see Prinzel standing in the doorway, a glass of wine in each hand. His eyes were fixed on the open drawer.

'I was looking for a piece of paper,' said von Igelfeld, slamming the drawer shut as he spoke.

It was clear that Prinzel did not believe him. 'But

why would you need paper, Herr von Igelfeld? Were you thinking of beginning an article for the *Zeitschrift* perhaps?'

Von Igelfeld laughed nervously. 'That would be very unusual!' he joked. 'One does not normally write an article at a social occasion!'

'Exactly,' said Prinzel. 'So why would one need paper?'

'I wanted to make a few notes,' said von Igelfeld. He tried to sound careless, as if taking notes in such circumstances was a matter of the slightest consequence.

Prinzel approached him with his glass of wine. 'On what?' he asked.

'A few lines occurred to me,' said von Igelfeld. 'One does not want to let these things escape. Pascal must have had a similar approach with his *Pensées*, don't you think? He must have jotted down the *pensées* as they occurred to him, otherwise he would have forgotten.'

Prinzel passed von Igelfeld his glass. 'Very commendable,' he said. 'So please allow me to find you some paper myself. It's easier, I think, for me to do it, as I know my way around my own bureau. And I would not want to put you to the trouble of searching through my private papers.'

Von Igelfeld felt himself blushing. 'I would never wish to read anything private,' he said. 'I hope that you didn't imagine that I . . .'

'Of course not,' said Prinzel. 'Look, here's a piece of paper. Please note down your thoughts before our other guest arrives.'

With a certain stiffness, von Igelfeld took the piece of paper that Prinzel offered him.

'And here's something to write with,' added Prinzel, passing a silver propelling pencil to his guest. 'Please go ahead. We can resume our conversation when you have finished . . . unless you're planning to write a whole chapter of notes, that is.'

'A few lines,' said von Igelfeld, scribbling casually on the piece of paper. 'There, that I think will suffice. I find that so many useful thoughts can be lost if one doesn't jot them down almost immediately.'

'Or if one is interrupted,' said Prinzel. 'Was there not an English poet who was composing an important poem when somebody knocked on the door? Did he not lose his train of thought?'

Von Igelfeld nodded. 'I believe that was Coleridge. I cannot imagine that the poem was of much value, of course – it would have been a different matter if somebody had knocked on Goethe's door. Then the world would truly have lost something.'

Prinzel agreed with this sentiment. 'Indeed, and now is that not the door bell? How fortunate that it should ring only after you have finished writing down your thoughts.'

Von Igelfeld smiled weakly. 'Indeed. Very fortunate, and fortuitous.'

Left alone for a moment while Prinzel went to join his wife in greeting Frau Benz, von Igelfeld folded the piece of paper and put it in his jacket pocket. Then, after nervously touching the hole in his trousers – it was not all that large, he decided – he chose a position near the fireplace where he could greet Frau Benz without sartorial compromise. It was a good place to stand because if invited to sit, he would be able to walk sideways to a nearby chair and lower himself on to it without displaying either of the holes.

A few minutes later, the new guest was ushered into the salon. Introductions were made, and von Igelfeld bowed formally to Frau Benz.

'I am most delighted to meet you, Herr von Igelfeld,' she said. 'I have heard so much about you from so many people.'

Von Igelfeld smiled. It was no great surprise, of course, that people should know about him; after all, he was the author of *Portuguese Irregular Verbs*, the definitive treatment of the subject. 'Ah!' he said. 'You have read my book, perhaps.'

Frau Benz looked blank. 'What book?'

Prinzel came to the rescue. 'Professor Dr Dr von Igelfeld has written a very important book, Frau Benz. It is called *Portuguese Irregular Verbs*.'

Frau Benz looked interested. 'Ah yes, I have seen that in the airport.'

'I do not think so,' said von Igelfeld.

'But I have, Herr von Igelfeld,' protested Frau Benz. 'They have all those language books for people going off on holiday to places like Portugal. Your book is among them . . . I'm sure.'

Prinzel laughed politely. 'Frau Benz is having her little joke,' he said. 'They would never sell Professor von Igelfeld's book at an airport, I'm afraid. It is not what you would call a bestseller.'

Von Igelfeld frowned. 'There are many libraries that bought it,' he said defensively.

'But Florianus is right,' interjected Ophelia Prinzel. 'Nobody buys your book, Moritz-Maria. That is not to say that they *should not* buy it. It's just that they don't.'

Frau Benz now made another contribution. 'There are many good books – very fine books, indeed – that are read by nobody at all. Perhaps Herr von Igelfeld's book is one of those. They can be very important books, but they are none the less completely ignored. It is undoubtedly very unfair.'

'But many people—' von Igelfeld began, only to be interrupted by Prinzel, who reached for a bottle on the table beside him and offered to refresh everybody's glass.

'Let us not worry about books, and who's reading them, or not, as the case may be. I, for one, have read Professor von Igelfeld's book and greatly enjoyed it.'

'And I shall read it too,' added Frau Benz, enthusiastically. 'When I next go to Portugal, I shall read it before I get on the plane and I'm sure that I shall speak perfect Portuguese by the time we arrive.'

'You would only be able to say things that required irregular verbs,' said Ophelia. 'And that might be difficult. One cannot claim to be really fluent in a language if one knows only the irregular verbs.'

The conversation moved on. Von Igelfeld gave Ophelia Prinzel a couple of reproachful looks for her unwarranted remarks on his book, but she did not appear to notice. It was all very well for her to talk about small sales, he thought, but what book had she ever written? And even to sell one or two copies was better than selling no copies at all – of a non-existent book. Hah! He would tell her that later, if the opportunity arose and the conversation returned to *Portuguese Irregular Verbs*.

He threw a glance at Frau Benz. She was a large woman, with what his mother had always described as a *generous front*. She was not tall, and indeed it crossed his mind that close measurement might reveal that she was as wide as she was high – perfectly square, in fact. Her hair, which was blonde, although a curiously faded shade of blonde, had been subjected to waving, and gave her a slightly sporting look, as if she might have spent some time gazing out to sea from the deck of a ship. Her eyes, which seemed somewhat small for her face, were none the less bright – *interested eyes*, thought von Igelfeld.

They finished their aperitif and went through to the Prinzels' dining room. As they entered, von Igelfeld noticed Frau Benz cast a glance around the room; well might one, he thought, if one lived, as she did, in the Schloss Dunkelberg. The dining rooms in that palace were immensely long, and it must seem strange to her that people could make do with such modest accommodation as this. Indeed, he wondered whether she might think that the Prinzels' dining room was in fact a cupboard; presumably there were cupboards in the Schloss Dunkelberg that were every bit as big as this.

Seated opposite Frau Benz, von Igelfeld decided to mention that he had visited her house.

'I must say, Frau Benz,' he began, 'that I find your house very charming. I had occasion to visit it – just as a member of the public. I was most taken with the ceilings.'

Frau Benz seemed pleased with the compliment, even if she took it very much in her stride. When one lives in such a house, von Igelfeld reflected, one must get used to people remarking upon one's ceilings. 'They are quite delightful,' she said. 'And I do hope that you will come and look at my ceilings again some time. I can give you a personal tour, if you wish.'

'I would enjoy that very much,' said von Igelfeld.

'And you can examine the new one I am currently having painted,' Frau Benz continued. 'It portrays a scene that is very dear to my heart.'

'And what would that be?' asked Ophelia.

'The apotheosis of Herr Benz,' said Frau Benz. 'My late husband is portrayed being welcomed into the celestial realm by St Peter, who is accompanied by a choir of well-known German personages, including Goethe and Wagner, of course.'

This was greeted with a silence that was eventually broken by von Igelfeld. 'I am most interested to hear of this project, Frau Benz. And how perceptive of you to discern that the heavenly realms are largely occupied by Germans. That seems to me to be entirely fitting.'

Frau Benz smiled sweetly. 'Thank you, dear Professor von Igelfeld. It is difficult to be sure about what lies ahead of us on the other side, but I had no difficulty in picturing this particular scene.'

'I have always imagined that heaven will look rather like Bavaria,' said Ophelia.

Frau Benz considered this. 'That is quite probably the case,' she said.

Prinzel looked doubtful. 'I do not think that we should extrapolate from what we know,' he said. 'If we are likely to find ourselves disembodied, then the actual surroundings of heaven may be similarly disembodied, do you not think?'

'No,' said Frau Benz. 'I'm confident that my artist will capture it perfectly accurately. And I do not believe that Herr Benz has been in any way disembodied since he left us. If anything, I believe that he may have put on weight.'

Ophelia now left the table to fetch the first course of soup. The talk flowed easily, moving lightly from subject to subject. Frau Benz proved to be an easy conversationalist – well informed and witty – and she and von Igelfeld appeared to get on very well. The soup plates were cleared and the next course served, all the while hosts and guests talking animatedly. Then there was cheese and biscuits, accompanied by small cups of strong coffee.

Frau Benz looked at her watch. 'Time has flown,' she said.

'Indeed it has,' agreed von Igelfeld. 'And there are so many topics that we have yet to discuss. It is ever thus, I believe.'

Frau Benz reached for the shawl she had hung over the back of her chair. 'Then we shall have to continue our conversation, Professor von Igelfeld,' she said. 'Perhaps you would care to come out to the Schloss Dunkelberg.'

Ophelia looked pointedly at Prinzel, who pretended not to have seen her glance.

'That would be very agreeable,' said von Igelfeld.

'Then shall we meet before too long?' asked Frau Benz.

Von Igelfeld nodded. 'That would be very convenient.'

'And if I might be permitted to mend your clothes,' Frau Benz went on, 'I'm a competent seamstress.'

Von Igelfeld blushed. 'That will not be necessary,' he muttered. 'But thank you, Frau Benz.'

Frau Benz was escorted to the door by Ophelia. Prinzel, having said goodbye to her, remained in the dining room with von Igelfeld. 'There you are!' he exclaimed. 'I could have told you, Herr von Igelfeld: you are a *gift* to eligible widows – a real gift!'

Von Igelfeld looked down at his shoes. 'Oh, I don't know . . .' he began modestly.

'And I must say, Herr von Igelfeld,' went on Prinzel, 'that was a brilliant stroke – coming in those clothes full of holes! That's exactly the sort of thing that tugs on the heartstrings of women. They can't resist the challenge.'

Von Igelfeld stared at his host. 'I don't know what you're talking about,' he said.

'Clever!' said Prinzel, wagging a finger at his friend.

'My goodness, Herr von Igelfeld, who would have known what a cunning . . . *Casanova* you've turned out to be. Who would have guessed?'

'Oh, I would.' This was from Ophelia, who had come back into the room after seeing Frau Benz off at the front door. 'I would certainly have guessed – because it's almost always the dull and boring ones who have hidden depths. Look behind the dry-as-dust exterior and what do you see? A Lothario! I've seen it so often – so often!'

Lunch at
the Schloss Dunkelberg

It would have been easy for von Igelfeld to make much of the invitation he had received to the Schloss Dunkelberg. He did not do this, however, but remained silent on the subject, beyond having a quiet word with the Librarian before morning coffee the following day. Prinzel, it appeared, had already said something to Herr Huber about the previous evening's dinner, and the Librarian was clearly excited by the subject when von Igelfeld met him in the corridor.

'So, Herr von Igelfeld,' he enthused. 'What is this I hear about your being invited to the Schloss Dunkelberg? What an honour!'

Von Igelfeld made a modest gesture of dismissal.

81

'Oh, I don't know, I really don't. But how did you hear about this matter, Herr Huber? Did Professor Dr Dr Prinzel . . .'

'. . . tell me? Yes, he did. He said that there appears to be the makings of a close friendship between you and the charming lady who owns the Schloss. And I am very pleased to hear it, I must say.'

Von Igelfeld was secretly gratified. 'Oh, I don't know about that, Herr Huber,' he said. 'We are certainly on good terms, but I'm not sure I would describe it as a close friendship. That is, perhaps, going a bit far.'

The Librarian appeared not to have heard him. 'It will be very pleasant when you are, perhaps, on even closer terms. I take it that we shall be able to call on you at the Schloss?' He paused. 'My aunt will be delighted to hear about this. She used to have a book of photographs of the Schloss, taken in the early days of the twentieth century. Not by her, of course, but by a well-known photographer, a certain Herr Noldt, if I remember correctly. You have perhaps heard of him. There is still a family of Noldts that's active in artistic circles, I believe.'

Von Igelfeld glanced about him. Laying a hand on the Librarian's sleeve, he addressed him quietly. 'I have not heard of Herr Noldt, but I shall keep an eye open for that book. However, I must ask you to be discreet about all this, Herr Huber. As you will understand, people like Frau Benz—'

'Is that her name?' interrupted the Librarian. 'It sounds strangely familiar. I wonder if my aunt . . .'

'Please, Herr Huber: what I was about to say is that in the circles in which Frau Benz moves, it is not thought to be good form to talk too openly about these personal matters. So I would not want, for example, Professor Dr Unterholzer, for all his many merits, to hear about this . . . just yet.'

Von Igelfeld was not sure exactly why he wanted to keep his meeting with Frau Benz from Unterholzer. One part of him wanted to boast about it – in order to put Unterholzer in his place. Unterholzer would never receive an invitation to view anybody's ceiling, let alone so distinguished a ceiling as that which sheltered Frau Benz. It would be satisfying, to say the least, to be able to remind him of that, but somehow to do so struck von Igelfeld as being in some way vaguely *dangerous*. Unterholzer was quite capable of spoiling anything, and von Igelfeld did not want to risk so delicate a plant as a budding romance by allowing Unterholzer to intrude.

Von Igelfeld had calculated that the Librarian would be flattered by being taken into his confidence, and this proved to be the case. 'Of course, Herr von Igelfeld,' said Herr Huber. 'You and I understand these things perfectly, even if not everybody . . .' and here he exchanged a conspiratorial glance with von Igelfeld, 'even if not *everybody* does.'

'Exactly,' said von Igelfeld. 'And thank you, Herr Huber. Thank you for your discretion – which, as ever, is much appreciated.' He paused. There were times when a small scrap of comfort had to be thrown to the Librarian. 'And tell me, Herr Huber, how is your dear aunt? I must try to visit her some day. Perhaps you and I could make a trip to the nursing home together.'

The Librarian beamed with pleasure. 'Oh, thank you, Herr von Igelfeld. That would be a very good thing to do. I could introduce you to the new matron, who is from Frankfurt, you'll be interested to hear, and very charming and well informed.'

Von Igelfeld smiled graciously. 'That would be very good. But perhaps we should not make any firm arrangements just yet, as I have certain obligations in relation to the Schloss . . .'

Herr Huber raised a finger to his lips in a gesture of solidarity. 'Of course,' he said, lowering his voice. 'There are more important visits for you to make. I understand perfectly.'

They were now at the coffee room door, and von Igelfeld noted with relief that although Prinzel had already arrived, there was no sign of Unterholzer. While the Librarian poured a cup of coffee for both of them, he approached Prinzel. 'Thank you very much for last evening,' he said. 'I enjoyed myself greatly.'

'So did we, Herr von Igelfeld,' said Prinzel. 'And so did Frau Benz, I believe.'

Prinzel made no effort to keep his voice down, and von Igelfeld frowned.

'Something wrong?' asked Prinzel.

'No, there is nothing wrong. It's just that I would prefer it if you could refrain from mentioning last night to our dear colleague Professor Unterholzer.' He looked at Prinzel imploringly. This was not a large favour to ask, he felt.

Prinzel shrugged. 'But I already have,' he said. 'I told him earlier this morning that you would be going out to the Schloss Dunkelberg some time soon.' He looked at von Igelfeld's expression of dismay. 'Have I spoken out of turn? I take it that this is not a confidential matter?'

'I would prefer it not to have been mentioned,' said von Igelfeld coldly. 'I wouldn't take it upon myself to mention your social arrangements to all and sundry.'

'Why not?' asked Prinzel. 'What does it matter who knows what I'm doing? It's hardly a state secret.'

'Not in your view,' said von Igelfeld. 'But not everybody . . .'

Support now came from an unlikely quarter. 'Not everybody likes to have their dirty washing done in public,' said the Librarian, handing a cup of coffee to von Igelfeld and looking defiantly at Prinzel.

'What's dirty about this washing?' countered Prinzel.

The Librarian stood his ground. 'That is just a metaphor.' He glanced at von Igelfeld, almost apologetically. 'I'm not suggesting that Professor von Igelfeld's washing is dirty, and certainly not dirtier that anybody else's. But you must remember that there are vulgar people who might wish to make something of his private life. Gossip columnists, for instance.'

Prinzel burst out laughing. 'I can't imagine for a moment that any gossip columnists would be the slightest bit interested in what Professor von Igelfeld gets up to, Herr Huber.'

Von Igelfeld looked at Prinzel reproachfully. He could not see why gossip columnists would *not* be interested. 'I don't know,' he began. 'There are people who might . . .'

'I don't think so,' said Prinzel firmly. 'What any of us does is of no conceivable interest to the people who read these things. They are interested in glamorous people – not in the likes of us. Not even Professor Zimmermann could expect a mention from those people.'

The conversation might have become even more acrimonious had it not been for the arrival of Unterholzer.

'This sounds very interesting,' he said breezily, as he helped himself to coffee. 'Gossip columnists? What about gossip columnists? Have they any interesting titbits for us in the newspapers today? Anything about, shall we say, new romances? Any new and exciting romances involving the chatelaine of a certain *Schloss*, shall we say?'

The Librarian gasped audibly. This was effrontery on a major scale; no wonder poor Professor von Igelfeld had wanted to keep this information from Unterholzer. But now it appeared that it was too late.

Von Igelfeld glowered at Unterholzer. 'I'm afraid that none of us is in a position to answer your question, Herr Unterholzer. As you will appreciate, we do not read the sort of newspaper in which such things are speculated upon.'

'We do not,' said the Librarian emphatically. 'Although sometimes when I am at the nursing home – when my aunt is perhaps having a bed-bath and I cannot go into her room for a few minutes – I sit in the waiting room and there are such publications on the table. It is sometimes inevitable that one will see—'

'Yes, Herr Huber,' interjected Unterholzer. 'We all know about that. But what about my question: any romantic news?'

Von Igelfeld did not deign to reply.

'Oh well,' said Unterholzer. 'Let's hope that those who make new, grand friends won't forget the rest of us when they get their knees under the table.'

Von Igelfeld glared at his colleague. It was typical of Unterholzer to use such a crude phrase: knees under the table, indeed. He imagined Unterholzer trying to push his own, rather large knees under an elegant, walnut-burr table – the sort of table that one might expect to find in every room in the Schloss Dunkelberg. It was not an edifying picture.

He decided to divert the discussion. 'Tell us, Herr Huber,' he began, 'about this waiting room in the nursing home. Does it face north or south? Or perhaps in some other direction?'

Von Igelfeld saw Unterholzer's eyes glaze over as the Librarian responded to the question. For the moment the threat had passed, but he would need to be vigilant.

Yet danger can come from an unexpected quarter, and it was while the Librarian was engaged in a long description of the waiting room that Prinzel suddenly interrupted him.

'Excuse me, Herr Huber,' he said, holding up a hand to stop the flow. 'That is all very fascinating but I have something to return to Professor von Igelfeld.'

Von Igelfeld frowned as Prinzel fished in his jacket and took out a folded piece of paper.

'Last night, Herr von Igelfeld, when you were at our house you dropped this piece of paper. You will recall that it was the paper on which you made some notes.'

Von Igelfeld looked in horror at the piece of paper.

'It's so easy,' Prinzel went on, 'to let things fall out of one's pocket – doubly so, if I might say, when one's suit has so many holes.'

Von Igelfeld said nothing.

'At first when I found this piece of paper,' said Prinzel, 'I had no idea what it was. There are some scribblings on it, but they seem to bear no relationship to any German words. I wondered if perhaps they were in an obscure language that I did not know. There are so many languages and so many scripts, one cannot possibly be on top of them all. What do you think, Herr Unterholzer?'

Prinzel handed the piece of paper to Unterholzer, who examined it eagerly. 'How interesting,' he said. 'I, too, find it difficult to decipher. What is this word here, for example? *Hutzzt*. That is a fascinating word. Or this one here? *Blah-blah*? That is very challenging.'

'Perhaps we should ask Herr von Igelfeld,' said Prinzel. 'I assumed that it was in code.'

Von Igelfeld leapt at the opening. 'That is exactly what it is,' he said.

Prinzel smiled. 'But why write in code?'

'Yes, why?' echoed Unterholzer. 'There is no need to write in code – none at all.'

'I read a book about the encoding machines once,' said the Librarian. 'It was by a mathematician who came from—'

'I'll tell you why I sometimes make notes in code,' said von Igelfeld, cutting through the Librarian's story. 'It is because there is always a danger that others – those with no authority to do so – will read one's notes. And that, as you see, sometimes happens.'

This remark was greeted with silence. There was something in von Igelfeld's tone that indicated that a boundary had been crossed. The silence persisted for the best part of a minute.

'So, if you'll forgive me,' von Igelfeld went on, 'I shall take my notes – thank you, Herr Prinzel – and return to my room.'

'Mathematicians are the best code breakers,' said the Librarian. 'I have always maintained that.'

Two days later a note arrived from Frau Benz inviting von Igelfeld to have lunch at the Schloss Dunkelberg the following Sunday. 'Nothing elaborate, I regret,' she wrote, 'but if the weather is fine we can eat on the west terrace. Very casual. I am very much looking forward to showing you the ceilings, including the ceiling that is currently being painted. I would welcome your input.'

Von Igelfeld was delighted to receive the invitation, even if slightly puzzled by the final sentence. He was not sure whether he would use the word *input* himself, and he was not certain quite what was expected of him. Were comments the same thing as input? He could always comment on the ceilings but if Frau Benz was expecting something more, then he felt that he would be unlikely to provide it. Although he was as interested as the next person in art and in questions of architectural design, he would hardly describe himself as an expert in this area. And he had never actually had any *input* in these matters, or at least not as far as he knew.

Then there were the words *very casual* to be considered. Did this mean that he was not expected to wear a tie? Or even a jacket? And if one did not wear a jacket, then should one roll one's sleeves up – a very plebeian practice, von Igelfeld had always felt – or perhaps wear a shirt that had short sleeves. He asked Prinzel, who said, 'Very casual means what it says. Certainly no tie. And yes, sleeves should be short, if the weather permits, which it looks as if it will.'

Von Igelfeld absorbed this advice. He did not think that he had any short-sleeved shirts, but it occurred to him that it would be a simple matter to cut the sleeves off a long-sleeved shirt. And the same could apply, he believed, if he was expected to wear short trousers, which again he did not possess: a quick snip of scissors to the legs of a pair of long trousers would quickly transform an unsuitable garment into a suitable one.

'Should I wear short trousers?' he asked Prinzel. 'Is that very casual?'

Prinzel thought for a moment. He had never seen von Igelfeld's legs, but he assumed that he had them, like everybody else. He smiled to himself as he pictured von Igelfeld in short trousers and a short-sleeved shirt. He would look very casual indeed.

'If the weather permits it,' he said. 'Yes, if conditions are right there would be nothing wrong in wearing short trousers to a very casual occasion. Indeed, the rule today, Herr von Igelfeld, is simple. Anything goes. That is the rule, I believe.'

'Schloss Dunkelberg, please,' said von Igelfeld to the taxi driver.

The driver looked at him in his rear-view mirror. 'Not possible,' he said.

Von Igelfeld stared at the back of the man's head. Was there something wrong with his car? 'Why?' he asked. 'I believe this is a taxi, and you are a taxi driver, if I'm not mistaken.'

He rather surprised himself with his boldness, and

even as he spoke he wondered whether the mistake was possibly his. A few years ago there had been an embarrassing incident in Munich when he had opened the door of a taxi, climbed in, and given his destination to the driver – only to discover that what he thought was a taxi was not one at all, but was the official car of the *Land*'s chief prosecutor. The prosecutor himself had arrived a few moments later, while his driver was still explaining to von Igelfeld that the car was not a taxi. It had been a *deeply* embarrassing incident, and von Igelfeld still remembered the looks of condescending amusement he had been given by both driver and prosecutor. It was their fault, of course: the car looked very much like a taxi, and they could hardly complain if innocent members of the public mistook it for one.

Now, as von Igelfeld glared at the back of his head, the driver turned round. 'Yes, this is a taxi,' he said. 'And I'm very happy to take you to your destination. But it cannot be the Schloss Dunkelberg, I'm afraid. This is Sunday, as you may have noticed, and the Schloss is never open on Sundays. That is why I said it was not possible, because it isn't. See?'

Von Igelfeld found the man's manner somewhat irritating. 'I *know* it's Sunday,' he said. 'And of course I know that the Schloss is not open to the public on Sundays. I, however, am not a member of the public.'

He said this with a flourish. There! That would put this man in his place.

The driver stared at him. 'You look like one to me,' he said.

'I look like what?'

'Like a member of the public. We're all members of the public, see. You, me, even the Chancellor. The Pope too, for that matter.'

Von Igelfeld pursed his lips. This was intolerable; one should be able to get into a taxi without becoming involved in a discussion of political and social philosophy.

'Family,' he said triumphantly. He did not think before he spoke, and it was perhaps not the best way of describing his role as a guest. But there was something so irritating about the driver that he felt he needed to convey very forcefully his special status in this visit. He was not quite family, of course, but he and Frau Benz had got on very well and there was every chance that in the fullness of time they might progress to first name terms.

'Ah!' said the driver. 'Why didn't you say so right at the beginning? I thought you were just an ordinary visitor, and I was trying to save you a wasted trip.'

'Well, there you are,' said von Igelfeld, sinking back into his seat. 'That is all settled.'

'Which entrance?' asked the driver.

Von Igelfeld thought quickly. He had previously

entered the precincts of the Schloss by coach – with the Regensburg Local History Society party – and he had not paid much attention to entrances. Having claimed to be family, though, he could hardly confess ignorance as to how one got into the Schloss. 'The usual,' he said.

The driver nodded. 'All right. I know the private drive well. I do a lot of driving for them, you know. Their own driver goes off on holiday from time to time and I step in for him. I know them all.'

He was looking in his mirror as he spoke, and he probably did not notice von Igelfeld's sudden stiffening.

'Oh yes,' said von Igelfeld. 'That is very good.' He paused for a few moments. 'Yes, very good.'

'I sometimes take Frau Benz shopping,' the driver continued. 'Is she your sister? She sometimes spoke of a brother in Frankfurt. That you?'

Von Igelfeld shook his head. 'No, that is not me.'

'What was his name?' asked the taxi driver. 'He was a *Graf* too, wasn't he?'

Von Igelfeld nodded, and looked out of the window. 'It has been very dry,' he observed. 'I hope it rains. The farmers will need it.'

The taxi driver shook his head. 'No, they won't. They've had enough. They think it's been very wet.'

'I see,' said von Igelfeld. 'Then I hope that it doesn't rain. I really hope so.'

'So are you a cousin, then?' asked the driver. 'Are you on Frau Benz's side or the other one?'

'It's very complicated,' said von Igelfeld. 'It is a very large family, and some of the members do not know one another, and have never met. That sometimes happens in very large, very formal families.'

'I see,' said the driver. 'Actually, I'd heard that. It's odd, though, isn't it? It's odd that members of the same family have never been introduced to one another.'

'That is the way it is in some circles,' said von Igelfeld. 'That is the way it's done.' He paused, before saying with a finality that he hoped would bring the conversation to an end, 'And it's not for us to question these things.'

The driver took the hint, and the rest of the trip was passed in silence. Sitting in the back of the car, von Igelfeld allowed himself to reflect on what would happen when he was the master of the Schloss Dunkelberg. He and Frau Benz – Frau von Igelfeld by then, of course – would entertain frequently – and handsomely. They would have a string quartet on call, to play in the north drawing room, and they would dine in the state dining room. He was not sure if there was a state dining room, but if there was not, there shortly would be one. It would be a very impressive room, with pictures of early von Igelfelds lining the walls, interspersed with Flemish tapestry scenes of hunting dogs and the like. And if there were no pictures of early von Igelfelds, that could always be remedied by engaging a suitable portrait painter to imagine what they might have looked like.

The library, of course, would be his redoubt. He would spend the mornings there, perhaps taking coffee on the terrace with Frau von Igelfeld at eleven o'clock. Then he would return to his desk, where he would work on his learned papers, a library table on either side piled high with leather-bound tomes. How agreeable that would be! And he might even do a bit of hunting in the woods surrounding the Schloss, inviting friends from Regensburg to join him – even Herr Huber! That would be highly entertaining: poor Herr Huber dressed in some absurd, ill-fitting set of lederhosen, with one of those odd hunting hats perched on his head! What a priceless image! And he would invite the Unterholzers too – and give them directions to enter by the tradesmen's entrance! That would be extremely amusing. The Prinzels, of course, would come in by the front drive.

And there would be possibilities for the summer, too, when the Schloss was open to the public. Von Igelfeld would be magnanimous in this respect, and would increase the number of open rooms, allowing visitors to get a glimpse of his study and perhaps even to see him working there. He would get up from his chair and welcome them personally, giving rise to breathless praise afterwards. 'And did you see how courteous the Graf was when we entered his study? Did you see how he allowed us to touch the leather bindings of those beautiful books? Such a kind man! Of course real aristocrats are like that, aren't they? They're not at all standoffish – it's the jumped-up arrivistes who come over all pompous. Real breeding always shows, you know . . .'

When they arrived at the Schloss, having swept up the private driveway that circled the elegantly laid out gardens, von Igelfeld paid the driver and they bade each other farewell with the polite reserve of a none-too-successful brief encounter. Von Igelfeld found himself faced by a large doorway that was surmounted by a stone coat of arms. He peered up at the arms – there was an owl, he thought, which was always reassuring. Owls, as symbols of wisdom, were a wiser choice for heraldic purposes than the more usual eagles or other birds of prey. Germany, of course, had an eagle as its symbol, which was not a particularly good idea, in von Igelfeld's view. A smaller, less aggressive bird might be more appropriate: a sparrow, perhaps, or a robin, neither of which seemed to feature very prominently in heraldry.

There was a bell pull, which he pulled with a sharp tug. It would take a long time, he thought, for a bell to sound in the depths of this great building, and an even longer time, he imagined, before anybody would come to the door. But there was no great delay, and within a very short time he heard a key being turned in the lock and the door opened before him. A small, grey-haired woman greeted him politely.

'Professor von Igelfeld?'

Von Igelfeld bowed. 'Yes. I believe that Frau Benz . . .'

'Oh, Frau Benz is certainly expecting you. She is very pleased about your visit. It is a great honour.'

Von Igelfeld beamed. The modern world was increasingly casual, and ill-mannered. People took others for granted and paid little attention to status. He did not consider himself immodest – far from it – but he *was* the author of *Portuguese Irregular Verbs*, and he was a respected professor of the University of Regensburg, and he did hold several honorary degrees, even if one was only from Belgium and another from an Italian university that had since closed down.

'The honour,' he said, 'is entirely mine.'

The woman smiled as she led him into an entrance hall. It was a room on a comfortable scale, with hunting prints adorning the walls, and a large rack for coats and hats. The only thing singling it out as a room in a *Schloss* rather than a mere country house was the height of the ceiling, and the elaborate plasterwork cornice that bounded it. And perhaps the carpets too, which were those faded Persian rugs of indeterminate blue that von

Igelfeld remembered from boyhood visits to his grandfather's house; the von Igelfelds did not live on quite this scale, but they need never apologise for the quality of their rugs.

The woman – a housekeeper, von Igelfeld presumed – led him through the hall and into a large drawing room. There, at the other end of the room, was Frau Benz herself, putting the finishing touches to a flower arrangement on a table in the window. She greeted him warmly, beckoning him across the room to admire the floral display.

'Every one of these flowers is from our own gardens, dear Professor von Igelfeld,' she said. 'My gardener has such a marvellous touch with flowers. He is perhaps less accomplished when it comes to vegetables – his heart, you see, is not in it; some gardeners are like that. But flowers are a different matter.' She paused. 'Is your own gardener good with flowers?'

Von Igelfeld shook his head. 'He is not,' he said.

He did not know why he said this. We sometimes speak without thinking, without meaning to mislead, and this was one such case. He should have admitted that he had no gardener – it is not a difficult thing to say: *I have no gardener* is not a statement of which anybody should have reason to feel ashamed. But he did not say this, and instead he heard himself say *He is not*.

'Then you should send him to my Herr Gunter,' said Frau Benz. 'He could spend a day with Herr Gunter and Herr Gunter would tell your Herr . . . What is your gardener's name?'

Von Igelfeld looked out of the window.

'Herr von Igelfeld? What is your gardener's name?'

'Herr . . . Herr Unterholzer.'

'Well then, you send your Herr Unterholzer to spend a day with Herr Gunter and he will come back to you knowing everything there is to know about flowers! What do you think of that idea?'

Von Igelfeld laughed nervously. 'A very good idea! I am sure that they would get on very well.'

Frau Benz now drew him gently towards the door. 'I know that you are interested in ceilings,' she said. 'So let's go and look at the ceiling I mentioned to you. The ceiling that depicts the entry of my dear husband into heaven.'

As they walked along a corridor that led off the drawing room, Frau Benz gave a further explanation of the ceiling. 'The concept, I must confess, is not original,' she said. 'Rubens painted a very similar scene, you know, in London. The Banqueting Hall in Whitehall has a ceiling depicting the apotheosis of King James I of England and VI of Scotland. It is a very fine painting which I have myself inspected on a trip to London.'

'It is better to see these things in person,' said von Igelfeld.

Frau Benz was in strong agreement with this. 'Exactly,' she said. 'There is nothing to equal the direct experience of being in the presence of great art. One can look at a photograph of a great painting and be moved, but one is never moved to the same extent as one is when one stands in front of the real thing. That is quite different.

'It was when I was in London, standing directly underneath Rubens' painting, that the idea occurred to me of portraying my dear late husband in a similar situation. That was the moment of insight; that was the moment at which I knew it was the right thing to do.'

'And it undoubtedly is,' said von Igelfeld.

She stopped when he said this and placed a hand gently on his forearm. 'Thank you, dear Professor von Igelfeld. You clearly understand about these things.'

'He was a great man,' said von Igelfeld. Again he had no idea why he should say such a thing; he had never met the late Herr Benz and knew nothing about him, other than that he was a manufacturer of some sort. But it seemed to him that to describe him in this way was the right thing to do, at least from the point of view of providing comfort to Frau Benz. She clearly missed her husband keenly, and to hear one whom one misses described as a great man must be a consolation, even if the tribute comes from one who might not have known much about the person so described, or might not have known anything about him, for that matter.

Frau Benz appeared to consider von Igelfeld's remark for a moment. First looking down at the floor, she raised her eyes slowly, and he saw her gratitude. 'He was,' she said quietly. 'None greater than he. Not one.'

'No,' said von Igelfeld. 'That is surely true.'

They were nearing the end of the corridor. A door led off to the right, and Frau Benz now pushed this open gently, with the air of one anxious not to disturb unduly what lay beyond. Momentarily awed, as if entering a newly decorated Sistine Chapel, von Igelfeld peered into the room beyond the door. The shutters were partly closed, which made the room dim, but there was enough light to make out the shape of a tower, of the sort used by painters and decorators, with a ladder strapped against its side.

Abandoning her guest for the moment, Frau Benz moved purposefully across the room and opened the shutters. In the flood of light that resulted, a long dining room was revealed, with walls covered with elaborate *chinois* wallpaper, and above that, only partly obscured by the painter's tower, the depiction, almost complete, of the apotheosis of Herr Benz.

'There it is,' said Frau Benz in hushed tones. 'Herr Benz being admitted to the heavenly realms – just as I imagine it took place in real life.'

Von Igelfeld stared at the picture. It was undoubtedly skilfully executed, in colours and tones reminiscent of the French Baroque. There was God himself, taking something of a back seat in proceedings, but emitting a divine glow that very satisfactorily illuminated the ranks of those angels hovering closest to him; and there were some of the figures from Germany's past: Goethe, still wearing his earthly clothes, von Igelfeld noted, and flourishing the very pen that must have written *The Sorrows of the Young Werther*, and Wagner too, flanked in his case by Rhine maidens. These buxom young women were pictured as beaming with relief; a relief that stemmed, von Igelfeld imagined, from having been translated from the murky realms of early German myth into these more luminescent, less riverine surroundings.

And finally, there was Herr Benz himself. He was unmistakable, being dressed in modern clothes – presumably the suit that he wore on his daily trip to his factories. Because of the angle from which he was viewed – an apotheosis being inevitably seen from below – it was possible to make out the soles of his shoes and the wine-red socks he was wearing. These details, von Igelfeld noted, were very finely caught by the painter, and he said as much to Frau Benz.

'Ah yes,' she said. 'His red socks. They were so important to him.'

They spent a few more minutes in the dining room before Frau Benz suggested that they move elsewhere. 'One cannot look at ceilings for too long,' she said. 'One's neck will not allow it.'

'Michelangelo must have had such a crick in *his* neck,' said von Igelfeld.

This witty observation was very well received by Frau Benz, who laughed appreciatively. 'I never thought of that,' she said.

Von Igelfeld felt almost light-headed as he tossed out the next remark. 'Well, I imagine that *he* did.'

Again, the witticism made Frau Benz laugh. And this, thought von Igelfeld, was beyond any doubt a good thing: it did not do, he felt, to contemplate deceased husbands *excessively*. Once they had been safely admitted to heaven, as Herr Benz clearly was, then one should perhaps consider *moving on*. There was very little mischief that one could get up to in heaven, particularly with Goethe and Wagner, not to say God, looking on, and so Frau Benz might well leave him there, so to speak, and concentrate on more earthly matters. He could not say this, of course – he realised that – but at least he could bring her out of herself with light-hearted conversation of the sort that he had now so spontaneously embarked upon. No, it

105

was going very well, he thought, and for a moment he imagined himself as the next male occupant of this charming *Schloss*, receiving some in one of the elegant drawing rooms, showing others the formal gardens with their playful fountains and elegant paths, so crunchy underfoot with their well-raked gravel. And at his side, supportive and admiring, would be Frau Benz herself, now – dare he entertain the delicious thought? – now Frau Professor Dr Dr (*honoris causa*) (*mult.*) von Igelfeld!

There was, of course, the question of whether a wife should restrict herself to being Frau Professor or whether she should include her husband's doctorates: opinion was divided on the matter, and there had been sharp exchanges in the German academic press. Von Igelfeld found himself uncertain, as he could see that each side of the dispute had something to be said for it. It could certainly be argued that to attribute doctorates to a person who did not have them was frankly misleading. Yet was this form actually doing that? If one thought about it carefully, to call a wife Frau Professor Dr was not actually suggesting that she had a doctorate; it was effectively denoting that she was the wife of a professor who *himself* had a doctorate. In that sense, there was no intention to deceive, and indeed no possible deception unless one were careless in one's interpretation of what was said. Of course some people were careless, and could misunderstand matters, and that was a powerful argument for holding that it was safer not to include the doctorate and refer simply to Frau Professor.

But then there was a further issue. What was the position if the wife of a professor had a doctorate in her own right? If one used the form *Frau Professor Dr* then there was a grave danger that people would think that the doctorate pertained to her husband and not to her. This situation could not be remedied by the simple inclusion of a further doctorate, as *Frau Professor Dr Dr* would surely normally be read as implying that her husband had, as was often the case, two doctorates. What, then?

Of course there were even more appalling complications. What if a woman who was herself a professor, and the possessor of two doctorates, were to marry another professor, *who had only one doctorate*? Von Igelfeld knew of no such case, but the fact that something had not yet occurred was no guarantee that it would not. If it did, then perhaps the only solution would be to call such a person Professor Dr Dr Frau Professor Dr. It was cumbersome, yes, but the fact that a term of address was cumbersome did not mean that one should shy away from it: exactitude, von Igelfeld had always maintained, was far more important than mere linguistic convenience.

He had put such thoughts behind him by the time they sat down for lunch on the west terrace. They were served by Ernst, a young manservant in a white linen jacket and black bow-tie. He brought them a consommé, followed by a concoction of fluffed white of eggs over which truffle-impregnated oil had been dribbled.

'A light lunch is always best,' said Frau Benz.

'Yes,' agreed von Igelfeld. 'The best sort of lunch is the lunch one sees photographs of these astronauts eating. It's so light it floats around the cabin.'

Frau Benz thought this very amusing, and complimented von Igelfeld on his wit. 'It must be wonderful to be able to make such funny remarks,' she said. 'What a great talent you have, Professor von Igelfeld. How you must make your colleagues laugh!'

Across von Igelfeld's mind there flashed a picture of morning coffee at the Institute, with Herr Huber going on about his aunt and the nursing home and Unterholzer rehearsing some grudge or other. It was not quite as Frau Benz imagined it; but then he felt different here, in her company: more vital, more appreciated, more capable of making diverting conversation.

'Oh, it's nothing, really,' he said modestly, but then added, 'Sometimes these things do slip out.'

'As they do from those writers of aphorisms,' said Frau Benz, dipping her fork into the egg. 'I assume they wake up each morning and wonder what aphorism will occur that day. I imagine that Friedrich von Schlegel's days began that way.'

'Or Marcus Aurelius and his *Meditations*,' said von Igelfeld. 'He presumably halted his campaigning in those melancholy fens if he felt a meditation coming on.'

Frau Benz rocked with laughter. 'Marcus Aurelius . . .' she giggled. 'A meditation's coming on . . .'

Von Igelfeld basked in the appreciative laughter. He looked out over the edge of the terrace. The ground sloped sharply away from the Schloss, and down below, so far below as to be a world in miniature, was a tablecloth of ripe fields: golden hay, wheat, oats: the lands of the Schloss. Distance precluded detail, but he imagined that closer inspection would reveal the presence of broad-beamed Brueghelian peasants, busy with their scythes, bringing in the harvest that would be translated soon enough into rents for the Schloss's coffers. How satisfactory, he thought, must the established order be when one is oneself well established within it.

They rounded off their lunch with coffee and small squares of chocolate-covered marzipan.

'I have so enjoyed myself,' said von Igelfeld. 'You have been most kind to me, Frau Benz.'

She smiled demurely. 'The pleasure has been mine, Professor von Igelfeld.'

He suddenly felt emboldened. 'And please, let's set

formality aside. I would be delighted were you to call me Moritz-Maria.'

It was a bold, perhaps reckless step to take, even if the invitation was hedged with an entirely appropriate subjunctive. Frau Benz was a person of conventional views; she lived in a *Schloss*; she was a respectable widow; one would not normally move on to first-name terms with such a person after no more than two meetings. A year, perhaps, would be about right; a year of formality before venturing – cautiously – into the realms of first-name intimacy. And here am I, he thought; here am I suggesting this after our very first lunch together. And lying about having a gardener too. So much, he reflected ruefully, for the von Igelfeld family motto, *Truth Always*.

Frau Benz hesitated, but only briefly. 'Thank you, Moritz-Maria, thank you. And please, I should be delighted if you were to address me as Kitty.'

'I shall be honoured to do so,' said von Igelfeld, thinking how fitting the name seemed. 'Kitty.'

They talked for a few minutes more before he glanced at his watch and told his hostess that it was time for him to go. 'Perhaps I could reciprocate by taking you to dinner,' he said. 'Would you by any chance be free tomorrow evening?'

She would, she said. And so the arrangement was made; they would meet at a French restaurant that von

110

Igelfeld had heard was very good and in line for the imminent award of a Michelin star. 'Stars are best appreciated before they come out,' he said.

Frau Benz looked thoughtful. 'That is a very engaging utterance,' she said. 'I shall have to think about its meaning. I suspect that it has many layers.'

'Like some Viennese cakes,' said von Igelfeld quickly.

They both laughed. The conversation had been brilliant, and it was entirely fitting that it should end on such a sparkling note.

He rose to leave. He had taken his jacket off – for the heat – and Frau Benz noticed that the sleeves of his shirt were curiously jagged. Perhaps it is the fashion, she thought; one of her nephews had rips in the knees of his jeans and she had been astonished to learn that the trousers had been bought that way and were often more expensive than those that did not have such tears. And here was Professor von Igelfeld, although no teenager, with shirt sleeves that looked as if they had been roughly cut with a pair of blunt scissors. Strange, she thought; very strange.

'Your driver will be waiting?' she asked.

Von Igelfeld was momentarily nonplussed. He had given no consideration to the question of how he would get home, having dismissed the taxi without making any arrangements for its return. 'My driver . . .' he muttered.

'I can ask mine to run you back,' said Frau Benz. 'I think he's still around somewhere. I'll call him.'

'That will not be necessary,' said von Igelfeld hurriedly. 'Mine will be parked outside the gate, I believe.' He paused. 'Under a tree.'

'Very wise,' said Frau Benz. 'Cars get so hot in the summer, don't they? Even good cars, like Mercedes-Benzes.'

Frau Benz smiled as she spoke, and von Igelfeld felt puzzled. There was something humorous, almost teasing, in what she said; but what was it?

'I do not particularly care for Mercedes-Benzes,' he said offhandedly. 'There are many other German cars that are every bit as good – and less flashy, if I might say so.'

Frau Benz stood quite still. For a few moments she said nothing. Then she opened her mouth and said, 'Oh?'

'Yes,' said von Igelfeld, searching his mind for something witty to say. 'I prefer a car that is less overstated. A Mercedes-Benz is fine for *nouveau riche* people, but for others, well, something less . . . less *shiny* is more appropriate. Or to have no car at all. That is the most fashionable choice, I believe.'

Frau Benz was silent, but had von Igelfeld looked at her, he would have noticed a slight quivering of the chin.

'No,' he continued expansively. 'I have no time for Mercedes-Benzes. None at all.'

112

Frau Benz moved very slowly towards the door. 'It was so kind of you to come, Professor von Igelfeld,' she said.

'Please: Moritz-Maria, Kitty.'

She appeared not to have heard. 'And I much appreciated your kind remarks about the ceiling, Professor von Igelfeld.'

Von Igelfeld felt his neck becoming warm. He wondered whether he had done something to offend his hostess; he must have – but what could it be? He looked down at his arms, at the shirt he had converted to short sleeves. Could it be that this amounted to some awful social solecism?

Frau Benz was opening the door.

'I look forward to our dinner,' said von Igelfeld, a note of anxiety creeping into his voice. 'I have read some very promising reviews of that restaurant.'

Frau Benz looked at him. 'Dinner? Oh, yes. I'm terribly sorry but I've just remembered that I have a dental appointment. We shall have to have dinner some other time. I'm so sorry.'

Von Igelfeld frowned. 'A dental appointment? But dentists don't work at night.'

Frau Benz looked away. 'We should never be too dogmatic,' she said quietly. 'About the hours that dentists work, or . . . or about other things.'

He stepped out. Behind him the door clanged shut,

a sound so final as to drive away all thoughts of living in a *Schloss*; of having a wife; of pursuing a life of quiet scholarship in a private library; of not having to listen to Herr Huber going on and on; of being somehow free in a world where freedom was a prize that most of us would never achieve, given that we were ourselves, and usually, if not always, had to remain ourselves for all our days, such as they were.

He frowned once again. Had he spoken out of turn about something? Women were unfathomable beings – even somebody as charming and pleasant as Frau Benz. She had seemed to be very taken with his witticisms – which had flowed quickly and easily for the entire visit – and then it was as if she had suddenly developed a headache. That was it: a headache. He would telephone her the next day and he was sure that he would discover that her good humour had completely returned. They would go out for dinner and then he would come back here for lunch, and all would be back to normal again. There was no need to worry.

He walked down the driveway towards the gate. It was not far from the nearest village and he could ask the people at the local inn to call a car for him. The exercise would do him good, he thought, after that excellent lunch.

There was a path off to the right – a short path that culminated in a paved stone circle on which a sundial had been erected. It was a most unusual sundial, von Igelfeld thought – a metal circle trisected into triangles: a strangely familiar symbol, but quite unexpected in such a setting.

Odd, he thought. Very odd.

Reading Party

A lesser man – one who, unlike von Igelfeld, had not written a twelve-hundred-page treatise on Portuguese irregular verbs – might have been cast down by such a rebuff as he received at the hands of Frau Benz. A lesser man, not having the history of the von Igelfeld family behind him – a history of insouciance in the face of adversity – might have become dispirited and might have thought that perhaps this social failure was his own doing. Not von Igelfeld: it was true that he felt a momentary disappointment at the frustration of his plans to marry Frau Benz and become the owner of the Schloss Dunkelberg, but this disappointment was moderated by the conviction that what the entire experience demonstrated was the unpredictability and inconstancy of women. And if that was the way that Frau Benz behaved, then he decided that he had had a narrow escape from marriage to such a difficult woman. It would have been all very well having the library at the Schloss Dunkelberg at his disposal, but what pleasure would it have been had he had to worry about what his wife would think and do next? There would be no peace in that, he thought; how much better to remain a bachelor and live in what was, after all, a perfectly comfortable flat with a view that, even if it was not of fertile acres of land which pertained to it, none the less encompassed a perfectly respectable public park. Frau Benz! Who had heard of the Benzes, whoever they were? Where were they in the sixteenth century? And as for the owl in their escutcheon – what a ridiculous device when compared with the hedgehog, whose role as an embodiment of wisdom was well known to anybody with even the slightest knowledge of iconography. And as for the apotheosis of Herr Benz – what an assumption to make that such a person, a mere manufacturer of whatever it was that he made, would be welcomed by luminaries of the voltage of Goethe and Wagner! It was quite preposterous, really, and he felt that he had shown considerable forbearance in not pointing this out to his hostess.

It was unfortunate, though, that Prinzel forgot all about von Igelfeld's request not to make much of the

Benz episode and asked a question that could only lead to embarrassment.

'How did your visit go?' he asked over coffee the following day. 'Plenty to talk about? Good look round – the Schloss that is?'

Herr Huber, who had just sat down, looked up sharply. 'Oh yes! Yesterday, wasn't it? And it was such a nice day for it. I said to myself: look at the sun, and just think that Professor von Igelfeld will be walking around the gardens at the Schloss, and will have them all to himself because the Schloss is closed on Sundays, to ordinary members of the public, that is. I thought that, you know, and then I thought that perhaps . . .'

Prinzel glanced at the Librarian. 'Very interesting, Herr Huber. But perhaps we should allow Professor von Igelfeld to tell us himself how his visit went.'

They looked at von Igelfeld, who was studying the rim of his coffee cup with sudden intensity.

'I had lunch at the Schloss,' he said. 'It was very pleasant being there without . . . without the public traipsing about.' He looked up as he mentioned the public and the implication could not have been clearer: Unterholzer, the Librarian, and even Prinzel were the very public whose absence was so welcome.

'Oh, I see,' said Unterholzer. 'A return to the days of exclusiveness. Perhaps there are those who believe that the public is best excluded from . . . from the Louvre, for example.'

'It would be a matter of great regret if that were to happen,' said Herr Huber. 'And I'm sure Professor von Igelfeld would not want people like us to be barred from the Louvre. But there is all the difference in the world, surely, between the Louvre and the Schloss Dunkelberg.'

'I don't see that at all,' snapped Unterholzer. 'Both are part of our artistic patrimony. They should not be just for the privileged. It's a matter of principle, no less.'

'Excuse me, Herr Unterholzer,' said the Librarian. 'But would you have turned down such an invitation?'

It was an unusually bold remark for Herr Huber, and for a few moments nobody said anything. Then Prinzel spoke. 'I don't think we should criticise Herr von Igelfeld unduly. What I'm interested in is the details of the visit. Was the conversation good? What did he see? What about the ceiling depicting the apotheosis of the late Herr Benz? These are the things that interest me.'

'I was shown the painted ceilings,' said von Igelfeld. 'Then we sat out on the terrace.'

Prinzel smiled. 'How very agreeable, I must say.' He paused. 'And will you be seeing Frau Benz again in the near future?'

Before von Igelfeld had the chance to answer, the Librarian chipped in brightly. 'I wonder if she drove you back in one of her cars,' he said. 'She must have a large fleet of them, I'd say.'

Von Igelfeld seized the opportunity to divert the conversation. 'Why on earth would she have a large fleet of cars, Herr Huber?'

'Mercedes-Benz,' said Unterholzer slowly. 'Benz.'

Von Igelfeld was silent. 'With a *z*?' he asked at last, his voice so quiet as to be virtually inaudible. 'I thought . . .'

'You thought it was spelled with an *s*?' asked the Librarian. 'Bens? That is unusual, but there was a nurse in my aunt's nursing home who married a Herr Bens. He came from Leipzig, I think. Yes he did, come to think of it, because I met him when they had a party for the staff and the nurse brought him along. He told me about Leipzig. They didn't invite everybody, of course, but they had a few relatives of patients, and they very kindly included me. People are so kind, you know, in these little ways . . .'

Von Igelfeld was not listening. He remembered his remarks about Mercedes-Benzes, and the way that what he said had seemed to impress Frau Benz into silence. Or perhaps impress was not the right word . . .

'And then afterwards,' continued the Librarian, 'a number of us went for a walk. I pride myself on taking

123

a reasonable amount of exercise, you know. People say that you should get about an hour or so every day. A lot of people find it difficult, and I can understand how they do. People in desk jobs, for example. Librarians, of course, get a lot of exercise – more than one might imagine. I find that. Putting books back on the shelves – that keeps me fit, even if I don't manage to get out and walk in the country. Picking up books and taking them to the shelves involves a lot of . . .'

'But you don't have many books to put back each day,' said Unterholzer. 'Two or three perhaps, because we're the only people who use the library, are we not? So if each of us takes a book once a day, this means that you have three books to put back. Forgive me for saying it, but I don't call that exercise.'

Von Igelfeld made his decision. These things happened, and occasionally one made a remark that was perhaps not quite as tactful as it might be. It was not his fault. How was he to have known that Herr Benz was something to do with cars? And, anyway, who wanted to live in a draughty *Schloss* halfway up a mountain? Flats were far more convenient.

'Exercise?' he said vaguely.

'Yes,' said the Librarian. 'Of course, you get a lot of exercise, Professor von Igelfeld, with the student reading party that you take up to the mountains each summer. Will you be going again this year, as usual? The students so enjoy it, I believe . . .'

Although von Igelfeld did not have a great deal of contact with the students who made up a large part of the population of Regensburg, the University encouraged the Institute to acknowledge – at least occasionally – its presence. After all, the University paid for the Institute, and von Igelfeld and his colleagues were appointed by it and were on the strength of its professoriat, even if the chief University officer, the Rector – whose official title was *His Magnificence the Rector* – was so rarely invited to Institute events that one of his predecessors had been actually unaware of the Institute's existence.

From the Institute's point of view, the requirements of duty were more than satisfied by taking on postgraduate students and guiding them through the writing of their doctoral theses, and by giving occasional lectures as part of ordinary University courses. Prinzel, for example, had recently completed a course of twenty-five lectures on western orthography – and this had proved highly popular with the students who attended it. Unterholzer lectured on vowels – to a very small audience, von Igelfeld noted – and von Igelfeld himself gave a major lecture on the development of Brazilian Portuguese which had been very well received by the student body. His real contribution, though, came in his leading of a small reading party during the summer – restricted to twenty places – that he had run for the last ten years. This reading party, which was intended for postgraduate students across the humanities, went each year to a small Alpine village where a University benefactor had built a comfortable lodge for precisely this sort of purpose. The reading element of this outing was perhaps less prominent than von Igelfeld would have liked, but he enjoyed the open air and the admiring company of the students, many of whom hoped that he might later be prevailed upon to provide an academic reference.

The popularity of this trip was a matter of pride to von Igelfeld, who had a tendency to claim the credit, even if what appealed to the students was the fact that the benefactor had established a trust that not only paid the expenses of every student attending but also gave each a token, but much appreciated, honorarium. Von Igelfeld, as presiding professor, received a considerably more generous honorarium that amounted to pure profit, as there was nothing to spend it on in the mountains and every conceivable expense was covered by the generous benefactor's trust.

Unterholzer, perhaps understandably, thought that the task of running the reading party should be shared. 'I see no reason why our dear colleague should do it year after year,' he complained to Prinzel. 'I'm sure that he does it very well, of course, not that I think there's much to do. All that it requires is making up a programme of discussions and then letting the students get on with it. Hardly onerous, if you ask me.'

Prinzel shrugged. He was not a jealous man by nature, and he did not see why the good fortune of a colleague should be so clearly resented. 'Moritz-Maria enjoys it,' he observed mildly. 'And he has so little else in his life, wouldn't you say? Don't you think it's nice that he gets at least one little treat like this?'

Unterholzer shook his head. 'I do not think that we should look upon this reading party as a treat,' he said. 'It is one of the few opportunities that the Institute has to influence the minds of the next generation of scholars. And that, I would have thought, is a most sacred task. No, this is not a holiday.'

'Then we should be grateful to him for shouldering the burden so willingly,' said Prinzel.

'But I am prepared to assist in that respect,' said Unterholzer. 'And what about you? Why can't you have a chance to lead the party for a change?'

Prinzel shrugged again. 'I'm afraid that I have no desire to disturb these arrangements,' he said. 'The students seem to enjoy themselves and there's always a waiting list for places. I think we should congratulate our colleague, rather than seek to replace him.'

The matter had been left at that, at least between

Unterholzer and Prinzel. But that did not prevent its being raised in the coffee room shortly before the party was due to set off.

'Off again to the mountains soon, Herr von Igelfeld,' said Unterholzer. 'My, you must know the way blindfold! You've been there so often.'

Von Igelfeld took a sip of his coffee. 'Yes, indeed, I am leaving in a day or two. But as for travelling blindfold, that is not something I would recommend, Herr Unterholzer, mountain roads being what they are. You must keep your wits about you at all times in the mountains, and keep a sharp eye open.'

'I was speaking metaphorically, Herr von Igelfeld,' Unterholzer retorted. 'However, I would also make the observation that familiarity has been known to breed contempt. So, for instance – and just as an example – if somebody were, say, to make a habit of taking every chance to go into the mountains, rather than sharing such opportunities with colleagues, such a person might perhaps become a bit careless. I'm not saying that he necessarily would, but there is the safety issue to be addressed. You know how aware people are of risk these days – especially when it comes to situations where one is in charge of young persons.'

Von Igelfeld considered this carefully before he replied. 'You are undoubtedly right, Herr Unterholzer. Such a person could become a bit blasé – that is perfectly possible; unless, of course, such a person were to be of a background that accustomed him to mountains. If a person came from a family with long roots in a mountainous region – such as my own family, for example – it would mean that he would be unlikely to fall into careless habits. One could not perhaps say the same thing for people who come from very low-lying areas . . .'

He left the last sentence unfinished, as the reference could not have been clearer. Unterholzer came from a low, potato-producing part of the country; one that was about as far as it was possible to be from any mountains.

Unterholzer bristled, but said nothing. It was clear that von Igelfeld was not going to share this perk and there was very little that could be done to dislodge him. Unless, of course, something went badly wrong, and one of the students was lost . . . No, he told himself; one should not even think of such a possibility. If it happened, though, it would teach von Igelfeld a lesson and surely it would be very difficult for him to continue to monopolise the reading party after that.

'There is a long waiting list for the reading party this year,' von Igelfeld continued. 'I have had a telephone call from somebody in the trust administration. She told me that there are eighty-seven students who wish to go to the Alps this summer. Eighty-seven!'

129

'That is far too many,' said the Librarian. 'You cannot take eighty-seven students anywhere. You would need a special train.'

'I am not proposing to take eighty-seven, Herr Huber,' von Igelfeld explained patiently. 'I shall take twenty. The rest will have to wait.'

The Librarian digested this information. 'Do you think it might be possible for me to come with you this year? The mountain air would do me good, I think, and it would be helpful for you to have an assistant.'

Von Igelfeld opened his mouth to speak, but found that no words came. How could he possibly take Herr Huber, of all people? He was a complete liability even at the best of times, on the valley floor so to speak, and he simply could not imagine the Librarian at higher altitudes. No, it was impossible.

'There is no call for a librarian in the mountains,' he said firmly. 'I'm so sorry, Herr Huber. Perhaps there is some other trip that you could go on.'

Unterholzer, who had begun to read a copy of the *Frankfurter Allgemeine*, now lowered his paper. 'I would have thought that there is no call for a professor of Romance philology in the Alps either,' he observed tartly. 'And yet you go, Herr von Igelfeld.'

Von Igelfeld pursed his lips. 'I lead the reading,' he said. 'There is every call for a professor to do that.'

'Or a librarian,' said Unterholzer. 'Reading, if I'm

not mistaken, involves books. And librarians have a certain expertise in that area, do they not?'

The Librarian, although grateful for Unterholzer's support, had no wish to provoke conflict. 'Perhaps I shall do something else,' he said. 'Although it would have been nice. Perhaps another year, if you are unable to go, Herr von Igelfeld, then I might be permitted to go. Perhaps as assistant to Professor Unterholzer.'

Von Igelfeld looked out of the window. He was not an ungenerous man, and he realised that he had a great number of things in his life that poor Herr Huber would never have. He had his book; he had his scholarly reputation; he had invitations to go to conferences; he had so much . . . The memory came to him of his great-uncle, a tall figure with piercing blue eyes, who always dressed in a dark green country suit that smelled of woodsmoke for some reason; who had taken him aside one evening when von Igelfeld was sixteen and had spoken to him about the duties of being a man. *Do not deny to others*, he said. *Remember that as a von Igelfeld, much is given to you. Give what you can to others who are not von Igelfelds.*

Herr Huber was decidedly not a von Igelfeld. Nobody was quite sure where he came from, as nobody had ever bothered to ask him. There was the nursing home that he spoke about, but that was hardly a *Heimat*, except to the unfortunates who resided there.

131

There was no Frau Huber, and no other relatives apart from his aunt, as far as anybody knew. And nobody knew where he lived, although Prinzel had once reported seeing Herr Huber entering a very small house on the edge of the woods.

'It was very strange,' he said. 'We were driving back one evening and just before you get into town proper there's an extremely small house, rather like the sort of house that you see Hansel and Gretel occupying in the opera. I had never noticed it before. Anyway, there was Herr Huber, no less, going in the front door. He must live there.'

Von Igelfeld remembered this as he looked back from the window. He thought of the librarian in his small house on the edge of the woods; he thought of him sitting in a small room in that small house. The memory of the words came back to him: *Give what you can to others who are not von Igelfelds.* Herr Huber was certainly not a von Igelfeld; he was just a Huber, and there were so many of them; *as the grains of sand are upon the beach, countless and without number.* 'Would you really like to come with us, Herr Huber?'

Herr Huber's eyes opened wide. 'Oh, I would,' he said. 'It would be so exciting.' His eyes returned to normal. 'But I understand that I cannot come and I shall be content to hear about it when you return.'

'No,' said von Igelfeld. 'You must accompany us. Your

presence would be a great help in so many respects. You could, for example . . .' He stopped. The Librarian looked at him expectantly, as did Unterholzer. 'You could look after the maps we use for our walks.'

'Of course I could,' said Herr Huber enthusiastically. 'I could file them away at the end of each day and get them out in the morning.'

Von Igelfeld nodded. 'That would be very useful.'

'And I could set up a system for storing the students' books,' Herr Huber continued. 'I've seen a picture of the common room at the lodge. I couldn't help but notice that the shelves were very badly arranged, with books all over the place.'

'There you are,' said von Igelfeld. 'You're already proving yourself indispensable.'

The day of departure arrived. Von Igelfeld travelled up to the lodge in a car provided by the trust, and since Herr Huber was now officially involved the Librarian travelled with him. The journey usually took four hours, and von Igelfeld had not been looking forward to spending that time as a captive audience of his colleague. Could anybody talk for four hours without disturbance on the subject of nursing homes and aunts, he wondered. The answer came to him immediately: Herr Huber undoubtedly could.

'I think that it might be best for you to sit in the

front, Herr Huber,' he said when they picked the Librarian up from his small house on the edge of town. 'I may need to do some work on the way up to the lodge, and that means I can spread papers out on the back seat. I hope you don't mind.'

The Librarian, who was brimming with excitement over the trip, indicated that this would not be the slightest inconvenience. 'And I can perhaps help with the navigation if the driver wishes me to,' he said.

'Of course,' said von Igelfeld. He should have warned the driver, he thought, but it was now too late and he would have to let events take their course; which they did, as the driver was subjected to a lengthy discourse on the relative merits of nursing homes in the Regensburg area. Poor man, thought von Igelfeld, closing his eyes in the back of the car; poor man to have to listen to Herr Huber. But no: the driver, it seemed, was interested.

'This is all very useful information, Herr Librarian,' he said as he negotiated his way through the traffic. 'May I tell you about my own experiences with my aged father? We kept him at home until it became really too difficult for my wife, try as she might.'

'A common experience, Herr Driver,' said the Librarian. 'I was talking to the son-in-law of one of the residents at my aunt's place only the other day, and he said that they—'

134

The driver cut him short. 'My wife has the patience of a saint,' he went on. 'She trained as a nurse, you know, and although she has been busy with the children and has not nursed for twenty years – no, let me work it out – we came to Regensburg from Mannheim when our youngest was three, and he's now twenty-seven, so that's twenty-four years, close enough. Mind you, as she herself says, "Looking after children – and a husband too – is a sort of nursing . . ."'

'Of course it is,' said the Librarian. 'I was talking the other day to a doctor – I think he came from Bielefeld originally – who said that we should not be making all these technical demands of nurses and should instead be trying to get good farm girls who have experience of looking after their younger siblings – they're the ones who know how to nurse. I said to him . . .'

And so it continued, for slightly more than four hours, until the car wound its way slowly up the last few yards of the steep driveway in front of the lodge.

'How quickly a journey passes when one is having an interesting conversation,' said the Librarian, as he got out of the car.

'How right you are, Herr Librarian,' said the driver. 'I do so look forward to our return drive.'

That evening, with the participants in the reading group all assembled in the lodge's common room, von Igelfeld made a short speech of welcome. Looking out over the faces of the twenty students, the Librarian and the couple of helpers from the trust staff, he drew attention to the challenges of the week ahead. 'This is a rare opportunity to spend time with those who share your intellectual interests,' he said, avoiding, as he said this, Herr Huber's enthusiastic stare. 'The whole point of going away on a reading party such as this, is to explore the minds of others. So make sure that you listen, as well as contribute, so that at the end of the week you can say to yourself: *I have learned something truly important.*'

There were nods of agreement from a number of students, while others expressed their approval of this sentiment by exchanging glances with their fellows. Moving on to deal with one or two administrative points, von Igelfeld then sketched out the shape of the week ahead. They would meet, he said, for two hours each morning to discuss their reading, and then the rest of the day would be free for private reflection and for walking along the paths that ran out in a number of directions from the lodge. These paths crossed Alpine meadow before becoming mountain tracks, not yet the preserve of actual climbers, but becoming so after a short while. 'Be careful,' said von Igelfeld. 'The mountains are a reminder to all of us that what goes up usually has to come down again!'

This amusing line, which von Igelfeld delivered slowly in order to allow the humour to be savoured, met each year with the same response, which came now: smiles from some of the students and open laughter from others. Von Igelfeld beamed: there was a unique pleasure, he felt, in finding oneself in contact with receptive young minds.

'And what comes down,' he continued, 'often does so rather faster than it goes up!'

This brought more laughter from the students, with one or two, he noticed, nudging one another. He inclined his head, acknowledging the appreciation of his humour, and then handed over to the cook, who wanted to say something about arrangements for picnic lunches, which could be ordered each morning from the kitchen.

After this, a glass of mulled wine was offered to students and staff alike, and von Igelfeld went round the room meeting the students. Although he selected them himself from the application forms presented to him by the trust administration, he tried to be as even-handed as possible, not favouring his own field, philology, above the claims of other humanities. So there were several classicists, a literary psychologist, historians and even a couple of artists. And there were men and women, with a slight bias this year in favour of men, although the opposite had been the case the previous year. Most were in their early twenties, which was compatible with the trust philosophy of helping those still engaged in full-time education and needing help at this tender stage of their academic careers; a few, though, were mature students in their thirties.

While circulating, von Igelfeld noticed that the students seemed to be mixing very well with one another. This did not surprise him, as reading groups usually spawned firm friendships that lasted beyond the week in the mountains, but that evening the atmosphere seemed to be particularly warm. In one corner of the room, a small group of students appeared to be getting on especially well, with shrieks of laughter and jovial patting of backs. He smiled at this: oh, to be twenty again! Oh, to be part again of a band of carefree brothers!

He turned to two young men who were standing near a window, looking out at the soaring mountain peaks beyond the glass. They introduced themselves politely: both, as it happened, were called Hans, and both were students of medieval French literature, although they had not met one another before.

'I have just come to Regensburg,' said Hans. 'I was in Berlin before.'

'And so now here we are: both interested in the same thing!' said the other Hans.

'That is the great delight of a reading party,' said von Igelfeld. 'One finds people who share one's interests.

And then, as the week progresses, one gets to know them better. It is very satisfactory.'

'We are certainly hoping to get to know one another better,' said Hans, smiling as he spoke. 'Would you not agree, Hans?'

Von Igelfeld left them to their discussion of medieval French literature – or what he assumed was a discussion of medieval French literature – and joined a group of four students – two men and two women – who had just finished talking to Herr Huber. He noticed that two of these seemed to be holding hands, although they disengaged as he came up to them. This was rather moving, he thought; that two young people, not much more than a boy and a girl, should already be encouraging one another in this way, allaying the intellectual uncertainty that must inevitably come from finding oneself in a reading group with so many other enquiring young minds. He smiled benignly at the couple, and they smiled back at him. It is very touching, he thought. Very touching.

Herr Huber appeared at his side. 'I must tell you, Herr von Igelfeld,' he began, 'that your words of welcome to the students were brilliant – quite brilliant!'

Von Igelfeld acknowledged the compliment with an inclination of his head. 'You are very kind, Herr Huber.'

'Yes, you were so reassuring. And now, look at these

splendid young people – look at them. They are already friends. See that boy over there talking to that girl in the green jersey. See how they have become good friends, and are already talking so earnestly about the reading that lies ahead.'

Von Igelfeld took a sip of his mulled wine. 'It is very encouraging,' he said. 'And it certainly cheers one to think that Germany is still producing these fine young people, with their strong intellectual curiosity and their thirst for knowledge. How fortunate we are, Herr Huber, to be part of that process.'

'Even if mine is a very small part,' said the Librarian.

Von Igelfeld turned to face his colleague. Poor Herr Huber, he thought, with his strange view of the world. 'But you must not be so modest,' he said, placing his hand briefly on his colleague's forearm. 'They also serve who merely stand and wait. You must remember that, Herr Huber!'

Herr Huber looked at von Igelfeld with eyes moist with gratitude. 'It is very kind of you to say that, Herr von Igelfeld. Sometimes I feel that . . . well, sometimes I feel that I have nothing to contribute. I am surrounded by such distinguished scholars – by you, by Professor Unterholzer . . .'

Von Igelfeld could not help a small frown crossing his brow at the mention of Unterholzer.

'. . . who is hardly your equal, of course,' the Librarian

continued, 'but who none the less tills, as you all do, an important furrow of scholarship.'

Von Igelfeld felt that he could afford to be generous. 'Yes, indeed he does. And even minor scholars have their place, as you have just pointed out. Yes, you are quite right, Herr Huber. But do remember: librarians are at the heart of the scholarly enterprise. Do not be too modest. You must join in our discussions in this reading party as a full and equal member.'

'Oh, I must not do that,' said Herr Huber. 'I shall be in attendance, of course, at all of them, and I shall most certainly assist in any way I can.' He glanced at his watch. 'But now, if you wouldn't mind excusing me, Herr von Igelfeld, I must go to my room and place a telephone call.'

'To your aunt?' asked von Igelfeld.

'To my aunt,' Herr Huber confirmed. 'You see, they are thinking of changing some of the rooms around at her nursing home. One of the ladies on the second floor fell out of a window and they want to put her on the ground floor now. That will mean that somebody will have to give up a room on that floor and move to the second floor.'

Von Igelfeld's eyes glassed over. 'To replace the defenestrated lady?' he asked distantly.

'Yes. But you know it's an interesting thing. You mentioned defenestration. I wonder whether that word

141

should be used to describe the act of falling out of the window by accident, or whether it should be restricted to those situations where somebody is thrown out of the window, as in the Defenestration of Prague. What do you think, Herr von Igelfeld? Have you given the matter much thought?'

Von Igelfeld looked across the room. Herr Huber was curiously tiring, even in these small doses. Did it matter how one was defenestrated? Surely from the point of view of the defenestrated person the significant feature of the experience was that one fell out of a window, not how one came to do so. He closed his eyes for a moment and saw, briefly but vividly, an image of Herr Huber standing beneath a window and looking up as a figure tumbled out above him. That, he thought, was an important aspect of defenestration that we should not forget: that it could be as dangerous to those below as it was to those above. But even if that were the case, one would not, he thought, use the word defenestration to describe what happened to the person on the ground below. If such a person were to be injured, then that experience could not be said to be a defenestration: it was a *consequence* of a defenestration. The distinction was important.

The welcome party over, they all had dinner together in the communal dining room. Von Igelfeld did not linger to chat afterwards, as the journey and the attenuated air of the mountainside had combined to make him feel sleepier than usual. He said goodnight to the students and nodded courteously in the direction of Herr Huber, who was engaged in animated conversation with a fair-haired woman, one of the older students, who von Igelfeld believed was interested in Irish drama. Herr Huber waved back in a friendly manner and returned to his conversation. Von Igelfeld smiled to himself; what on earth could that young woman be discussing with the Librarian? Should he go to her rescue and allow her to detach herself from Herr Huber and his monologue? He decided against this; the woman looked as if she was in her thirties somewhere and would clearly be capable of looking after herself. She would no doubt find some excuse to escape Herr Huber when she felt that she could bear his conversation no longer.

As director of the programme, von Igelfeld was entitled to – and had claimed – the best room in the lodge. Although some of the students were doubled up, von Igelfeld and the Librarian did not have to share. It would have been impossible to occupy the same room as Herr Huber, von Igelfeld felt; a recipe for a nightmare – every night. The Librarian would no doubt talk in his sleep – about much the same thing that he talked about when awake, and that would be insupportable.

His own room was in the front of the building, and afforded an unobstructed view of Alpine pasture and mountains. As he prepared for bed, he looked towards the mountains; the moon was full and he could make out the white of the snow-topped peaks. He shivered. He was not a creature of raw nature; he was one for the warmth and security of villages, towns, cities. It astonished him to think that even as he looked out at those peaks there were climbers bivouacked up there, huddled in their flimsy tents, clinging to the tiny ledges where if one rolled over in the wrong direction one might plunge, sleeping bag and all, down into some bottomless abyss.

He went to bed, reading for ten minutes or so before drowsiness overcame him and he turned out the light. At some point in the night he dreamed that he was in a towering building, so high that the roof was shrouded in a blanket of snow. He was in a room, looking out of a window, and there was somebody behind him. He opened the window, the better to see outside, but he could make out little because of low cloud that had descended to envelop the building. He turned round; somebody was addressing him. Unterholzer.

'Defenestration,' said Unterholzer menacingly. 'Defenestration.'

Von Igelfeld cried out, but there was nobody to hear him except Unterholzer, who was now advancing upon

144

him, forcing him to move towards the open window. And then, with a sudden movement from Unterholzer, von Igelfeld was defenestrated.

He awoke, sweating with anxiety. He looked at his watch: it was shortly after three, a bad hour to awaken. He reached for his glass of water, and found that it was empty.

Rising from bed, he made his way out into the corridor and began to walk towards the bathroom. He heard a noise, and turned round sharply. Somebody had come out of one door, lingered for no more than a moment or two in the corridor, and then slipped back into another door. Von Igelfeld wondered what was happening. Perhaps the students were continuing their conversation from the common room; students liked to stay awake, von Igelfeld remembered. In his own day in Heidelberg they sometimes chatted away until two or three in the morning, and would think nothing of staying up until five at weekends.

He filled his glass with water and returned to his room. As he closed the door behind him, he heard a door opening in the corridor, and then the sound of whispering. He put down the glass and returned to the door. Bending down, he looked through the keyhole. There was a movement, blurred and indistinct in the half-light of the corridor, and then nothing. He turned away. Young people! Perhaps they were playing some sort of party game; he had read recently of a game called *sardines* that young people played, in which one person went off to hide and others then crept about the house, finding the hiding place and attempting to join the person crouching there. It was such a ridiculous game, and yet it was, apparently, very popular. Perhaps he should ask them at breakfast tomorrow. 'And who was playing sardines last night?' he might say, with the air of Hercule Poirot in full investigation; that would show the students that he was on top of what was going on.

The first discussion period followed breakfast the next morning. The theme of the discussion was a very general one, so designed as to ensure that everybody had a chance to contribute views. The topic – 'Should language be allowed to evolve naturally or should it be regulated by a national academy, such as the Académie Française?' – caused a great stir. Most of the students agreed that language should be left to evolve naturally, although one or two purists took strong exception to this. The Académie Française, they said, deserved everybody's thanks for standing up against the relentless tide of Anglo-Saxon linguistic pollution that was infecting so many languages. Von Igelfeld agreed, but said nothing: this debate was for the students, and one could hardly expect students to reach the right conclusion about

146

anything. In illustrating their point, one or two of the students in favour of linguistic freedom used words that he did not quite understand, but he did not reveal this: such words were inevitably vulgar and would be forgotten after a year or two, like that American word *okay*, which he had always felt would never last once the novelty wore off. Or *vachement* in French: what a ridiculous neologism that was: one would certainly not hear that in the halls of the Académie Française!

At the end of the discussion coffee was served. Von Igelfeld announced that he and the trust administrator would be available afterwards to resolve any administrative issues or deal with any queries about the programme.

'My door is always open,' he announced, and then quipped, 'Except, that is, when it is clearly closed.'

This brought smiles of appreciation from the students, and von Igelfeld basked in their approbation. Perhaps students were not such a nuisance after all; perhaps the Institute should consider having a few more – not too many, of course; an extra three or four a year might be about right. He would take that up with Prinzel, he thought, on his return, and then, if the two of them agreed, they could present the decision as a *fait accompli*, or even a *fait vachement accompli*, to Unterholzer. He smiled at the linguistic joke, and wished that he could share it with somebody who would understand. He glanced about him – Herr Huber? No, he was deeply engrossed in conversation with that same young woman he had been talking to the previous evening. Poor young woman, von Igelfeld said to himself. Perhaps I should have a private word with Herr Huber and tell him that he shouldn't burden her too much with his conversation.

He sat down with the administrator and waited to deal with the first of the students who had indicated that they had an admininstrative issue. This was one of the young men called Hans whom von Igelfeld had spoken to briefly before dinner the night before.

'I take it that everything is going well,' said von Igelfeld as the young man sat down in front of him.

'Oh, yes, Herr Professor. It certainly is.'

Von Igelfeld nodded. 'Is there anything we can do for you?'

The young man looked down at the floor. 'I was wondering whether it might be possible to change rooms,' he said. 'I'm sharing with Georg over there and I'm afraid that he snores. It's very difficult to sleep if somebody is snoring.'

'Of course it is,' said von Igelfeld. 'Certainly you can change.'

The adminstrator glanced at von Igelfeld. 'Accommodation's very tight,' he said. 'I don't think we have anything available.'

Hans looked at von Igelfeld. 'But I have had an idea,

professor,' he said. 'I could share with the other Hans. He says that he would be very happy to share with me, to save me from Georg's snoring.'

The administrator looked at his list. 'But he has a single room. There is only one bed in that room.'

'We don't mind,' said Hans hurriedly. 'Hans is not very large and there will be room.'

The administrator frowned. 'I'm not sure that . . .'

'Fine,' said von Igelfeld. 'That is very kind of him. You are lucky to have such a generous friend. And at least you will get plenty of sleep now – unless other Hans snores!'

Hans beamed with pleasure. 'No, he doesn't. I can tell you . . .'

'Good,' said von Igelfeld.

The next student was a young woman. She, too, wanted to change rooms, and had heard that there might be a chance of getting the bed previously occupied by Hans.

'But that room is already occupied by Georg,' said the administrator.

'That's fine,' said the young woman. 'I've spoken to him and he says that he doesn't mind.'

The administrator looked at von Igelfeld. 'This is very irregular, Professor von Igelfeld,' he whispered. 'We do not put male and female students in the same room. We have never done that. Otherwise . . .'

Von Igelfeld ignored the administrator and turned to the student. 'You are a friend of this young man, are you?'

The student smiled at him. 'We are friends. We read to each other, you see, and it would be nice to be able to do that here.'

'Of course it would,' said von Igelfeld. 'It is very useful to have somebody to read to one when one's eyes are tired.'

The administrator tried to interrupt. 'I'm not sure that policy allows . . .'

'Don't worry about that,' said von Igelfeld. 'I shall authorise this.'

There were several other requests made that morning, all concerned with moving rooms. The administrator became quite sulky. 'Once this starts,' he complained to von Igelfeld, 'it will never end. With the greatest respect, Professor von Igelfeld, in previous years I have handled all the accommodation issues myself, without troubling you. Now that you are taking an interest in them, I'm afraid that it is all going to become excessively complicated.'

'I do not see that,' said von Igelfeld. 'These young people need to be comfortable so that they can apply their minds to the discussions. It is important that they get sound sleep.'

The administrator stared at him incredulously. He

hesitated for a while before replying, as if weighing his words carefully. 'I'm not sure if you appreciate what is happening here, Professor von Igelfeld. The reason why the students are interfering with my perfectly good accommodation arrangements is that they are up to—'

He did not finish. 'Excuse me, Herr Wolters,' said von Igelfeld icily. 'I am perfectly aware of what's what. But thank you very much for your concern, which is, as always, much appreciated.'

He looked about him in irritation. Really! It was intolerable that mere administrators should think fit to question professorial judgement. He had heard that this had been happening more and more in universities, but he would certainly resist it when he came across it, as he now did. What next? Would it be librarians who started to throw their weight around? Herr Huber telling *him* what to do?

Where *was* Herr Huber? Perhaps he should have a word with him and check up that the filing of the maps was in order. Herr Huber, for all his wittering on about all sorts of ephemera, was a highly conscientious librarian and would certainly have filed the maps by now, but seemed to be out of the room. Von Igelfeld rose to look out of the window. He spotted Herr Huber immediately, walking towards a cluster of pine trees with that same young woman. Von Igelfeld sighed; he could just imagine the conversation. 'There are some pine trees remarkably like this in the grounds of my aunt's nursing home, you know. I drew the attention of the matron to them and she explained that . . .'

The next few days passed without incident. There were some very successful discussion sessions, and two lengthy book reports prepared by students chosen by von Igelfeld for this honour. There were also several most enjoyable hikes, in which the entire party participated, even Herr Huber, who was wearing, much to von Igelfeld's amusement, traditional Bavarian lederhosen.

'I fear your knees will feel somewhat cold,' said von Igelfeld. 'But it's your choice, Herr Huber. I would never presume to comment on a colleague's clothing, even if he were to look ridiculous.'

'You are very kind,' said Herr Huber, as they strode along. 'I must say that I enjoy wearing this outfit, which belonged to my late uncle, you know. He has nothing to do with the aunt you may have heard me refer to; he is on the other side. He lived in Berlin for many years, you know, and . . .'

'Yes, yes, that is all very interesting, Herr Huber, but I was wanting to speak to you about a more delicate matter. I don't think that one should monopolise the time of any of the young people who are with us, don't you agree?'

'I most certainly agree,' said the Librarian.

'So you should perhaps give that young woman a bit of a break from your company,' said von Igelfeld.

Herr Huber's tread faltered. His knees, visible below the edge of his lederhosen, seemed to tremble slightly. 'But I cannot be unkind to her,' he said. 'She keeps seeking out my company and we get on very well.'

'*She* seeks *you* out?' asked von Igelfeld.

Herr Huber nodded. 'And her own company is very delightful. Look, here she is now.'

Herr Huber's friend came striding towards him. 'Stoffi, come on. Let's go and walk at the front. Come along.'

Von Igelfeld looked on in astonishment as the Librarian's arm was taken and he was led away to the front of the walking party. Stoffi! He had never before heard anybody call the Librarian by his first name, and he was appalled that a student should presume to do so. It was true that she was a post-graduate student, and clearly into her thirties already, but she was still technically a student and therefore of a distinctly lower academic rank even than that occupied by Herr Huber. And he was also astonished at the way she took Herr Huber's arm; it was almost as if there was something between them – an intimacy even – which of course was frankly unbelievable and need not be thought about any further. Stoffi! Well, none of them would ever dare to call him Moritz-Maria – that was as firm as the very rocks on which they were now walking, high above the distant valley, high in an air that seemed so sweet and pure that to breathe it was to purge the lungs of all staleness and despair. He would rise above these petty matters, he decided, and enjoy the mountain air to the full. He breathed in; it was delightful, quite delightful. He felt content. The problems of the world are far away, he thought, and they need not worry me here. He paused. What exactly were the problems of the world? They were profound, he was sure, but he now realised that he had not exactly exercised himself over them during the past few years. Nor before that either. In fact, he had never really considered them at all, and he decided that now he should perhaps do so. Linguistic pollution? The decline of the subjunctive? The intrusion of English words into Romance languages? This was the sort of thing that the world needed to get to grips with, and he would not flinch in the face of such issues.

He slipped into a most agreeable routine that included an early morning stroll immediately after breakfast and a more ambitious hike in the afternoon. The morning stroll was usually a solitary affair, taken while the students had their morning discussion, in which he used the time by himself to think about the various scholarly projects that he had lined up for the autumn and winter. The possibility of a new edition of *Portuguese Irregular Verbs* had been raised by the chairman of the Max-Planck Foundation and von Igelfeld was now giving it serious consideration. The chairman's letter had been persuasive: *We are interested in funding the publication of a series that will include the twenty or so most significant works of scholarship in a widely varying range of disciplines. These will be books that are already in print, or that have been in print but are now out of print. They will be, quite simply, the crowning glories of German scholarship of the second half of the twentieth century and the first part of the twenty-first. They are books that will endure in the manner that Horace anticipated for his* Odes.

Von Igelfeld had taken considerable satisfaction from the terms of this letter. He knew what Horace had written about his *Odes* – '*Exegi monumentum aere perennius*: I have created a monument more lasting than bronze.' It was not the most modest of comments on one's own work, perhaps, but it was the chairman who had brought it up and not von Igelfeld, and it was hardly immodest to contemplate the compliments passed by others. The appropriate response to such a compliment was to acknowledge it with a slight bow of the head, which von Igelfeld had, in fact, done when he had first read the glowing sentence.

Now, in the mountains, he was able to use the

tranquillity of the winding paths to think about how he would tackle the writing of a second edition and of what new material he would incorporate. And there were other things, too, that needed to be thought about: a paper to be delivered in Sweden in November at an important conference of Romance philologists – this would have to be written by the middle of October as it was to be included in the published proceedings of the conference. Then there were several books for review in the *Zeitschrift* – not an unduly onerous task, but one that would none the less require weeks of work. Yes, he thought, the *monumentum aere perennus* was still a work in progress.

It was towards the end of the week that von Igelfeld set off for a morning stroll rather earlier than usual. He had risen shortly after six, having left his blind slightly open and thus allowed the morning sun to stream directly into his room. This had woken him up and taken him to the window to gaze out on a morning of quite exceptional beauty. Opening the window, he stuck his head out and breathed in the champagne-like air. It was quite exhilarating and it inspired him to have his walk before breakfast rather than afterwards.

Dressed in his mountain-walking clothes – plus-twos, green knitted socks, a pair of stout climbing boots, and a waterproof jacket – von Igelfeld strode out of the lodge and on to a path that he had not taken before.

This path was considerably steeper than most of those that ran from the lodge and was generally thought to be a little too ambitious for those unused to Alpine conditions. Von Igelfeld, however, felt that the week's practice he had already had equipped him perfectly well for a short walk along this path. If conditions became too difficult he could always turn back; there was no danger.

He walked for fifteen minutes or so. The path rose sharply and there were several points at which he was obliged to clamber rather than walk. It was good exercise, though, and he felt pleased that the level of fitness he had already achieved made it relatively easy for him to cope with the exertions involved. Unterholzer would never manage this, he thought, not without some satisfaction.

Coming to a point where his path converged with another, von Igelfeld decided to take a rest. He sat down on a smooth rock and looked out across the valley below. Then, turning round, he peered up at the mountain behind him. It seemed impossibly high, and he felt dizzy just from looking up at the needle-like crags so high above him.

He was disturbed by the sound of voices. 'Here, I think. Perhaps a five-minute break . . .'

He looked round. A party of mountaineers – ten in number – had arrived by the other path and were looking about for places to sit down and rest. Their leader, a tall man dressed entirely in green, smiled at von Igelfeld and came over to greet him.

'Ah,' said the leader. 'We were expecting you.'

Von Igelfeld inclined his head and introduced himself. 'Von Igelfeld,' he said. 'Regensburg.'

'Of course,' said the leader. 'We know several members of your club. We climbed in Spain last year.'

Von Igelfeld was puzzled. Club? He was about to enquire what club was being referred to when the leader asked him, 'Are you happy to join us today? We're going up there.' He tossed his head in the direction of the towering mountainside above them.

'Oh, I'm not sure,' said von Igelfeld. 'I'm not all that experienced.'

The leader laughed. 'You're very modest,' he said.

'Perhaps,' said von Igelfeld. 'But I'd be happy to come part of the way.'

The leader nodded. 'That's fine. You can come down again whenever you like. There are some fixed ropes on that face over there – I used them a few months ago. You'll be all right with those.'

Von Igelfeld looked in the direction in which the leader was pointing. The rock seemed almost vertical there, but he could turn back well before they reached that point. And it would be good to walk with these agreeable-sounding people, even if only for half an hour or so.

They rested for a few minutes more before setting off again. They were roping together now, and a kind woman in a red jersey helped von Igelfeld to clip up. 'I'm not surprised you find these clips difficult,' she said. 'Stefan introduced them. They're a new design. Very tricky, but very safe.'

'It's best to be safe,' said von Igelfeld. 'There can be no doubt about that.'

'Exactly,' said the woman. 'Ever since we lost Martin we've been ultra-careful.'

'I'm sorry to hear about that,' said von Igelfeld. 'He had an accident?'

The woman looked down at the ground. 'He was a little bit foolhardy,' she said. 'I know that nobody likes to say that now – not after what happened – but the truth of the matter is that if he hadn't climbed beyond his competence he'd be with us still.'

Von Igelfeld absorbed this information as they began to make their way up the mountain. The path had all but disappeared and they were advancing across an alarmingly steep field of scree. Small rocks, dislodged by the boots of the climbers, rolled down the hill, gathering others as they did so. The noise made by these tiny landslides, although a danger to nobody, seemed ominously loud to von Igelfeld. He wondered whether that was the sound that a person would make if he were to fall. Was that the sound that poor Martin made when he tumbled? Or would a person fall more soundlessly, at least during the fall itself, until there came a dull thud at the end?

He made a conscious effort to stop these morbid thoughts and instead to enjoy the fact that he was now engaged in what appeared to be real climbing, with real mountaineers. He would be able to report this to the students when he returned to the lodge. He would not be boastful, of course, but he would certainly mention that they had been roped together. That would definitely impress.

After traversing the scree, the lead climbers turned and began to make their way up a steep face of rock. Von Igelfeld, roped to the woman in the red jersey who was directly in front of him, watched what she did and followed suit slavishly. It was not too difficult, he found, and he simply had to use the cracks in the rock that she used to place her hands and her feet. If this was mountaineering, then even if it was not exactly easy, it was not as difficult as it looked. The important thing, he decided, was not to look down. He had snatched the occasional glance earlier on, but had rapidly looked away; now, as they made their way up the face, he stared resolutely ahead.

There were further faces, and each of them he negotiated successfully, following the lead of the woman in front of him. She proved to be a safe and methodical climber, and a good tutor too. 'You're doing very well,' she encouraged him. 'If you continue like this, then you'll make the summit with no difficulty.'

Von Igelfeld looked at his watch and frowned. They had been climbing for almost two hours now, and they were high above the point at which he had met the group. If he turned back now, how would he be able to get back by himself? He decided to ask his tutor.

'Impossible,' she said. 'You couldn't do it by yourself. Out of the question. You'll have to continue.'

Their progress was slower now, as there were points of real difficulty in that part of the ascent. At one stage he slipped, but did not lose his footing and was immediately caught by his climbing companion. They were now on ice, with large patches of snow on either side of them.

'Be careful here,' she said. 'Ice can be so treacherous.'

Von Igelfeld swallowed hard. 'Treacherous,' he muttered.

'That's what got poor Martin,' said the woman.

'Ice?'

'Yes. Ice. Just like this.'

Von Igelfeld laughed. 'Ice holds no fears for me,' he said. 'I have dealt with ice on many occasions.'

'You never know with ice . . . .' the woman began.

'Courage,' said von Igelfeld firmly. 'Courage is what

counts. If you have that, then a climb like this is nothing to worry about.'

The woman looked doubtful. 'Even the best—' she said.

'And determination,' interjected von Igelfeld. 'I've always said that the most important thing in mountaineering is *attitude*. If you have the right attitude, then you can deal with everything the mountain confronts you with.'

The woman was silent.

'So, I suggest we press on,' said von Igelfeld. 'I am enjoying this climb immensely and am confident that we shall reach the summit in no time at all. Attitude – as I have said – is what counts.'

They reached the summit shortly after two in the afternoon. Von Igelfeld by that stage was utterly exhausted, but felt an immense surge of pride as he shook hands with his companions. He had climbed a high and important mountain; he had not just been for a mountain hike as all the others were doing; he had actually *climbed*. And it had not been difficult at all: one simply watched the person in front of one and did what that person did. One might even ascend Everest in this way; he had heard that there were guides who would take you up even if you were not particularly experienced. Perhaps he could do that next. This mountain, which he had been told by the woman in the red jersey was called the Devil's Needles, could be the preparation for Everest itself, or perhaps that other one, K2, or whatever it was called. This could be K1, in the same way as Mozart's first work must have been K1. He smiled. Did Köchel number mountains as well as symphonies? That was a splendid joke, and he was about to tell it to the woman in the red jersey when he slipped and fell, right at the edge of the flat landing that made up the summit.

It happened very quickly. He sensed that his legs were going from under him – a sheet of ice, of course – and then he felt himself sliding. He heard shouts and he saw a blur of red. He slid and seemed to gather momentum; they had unroped at the top and there was nothing to stop him. He started to fall now, and suddenly was airborne, even if only briefly. He came down, landing on snow that felt much harder than it looked. He tumbled, head over heels now, and was airborne again. Beneath him, nothing, an abyss; trees flashed past, sky, flat expanses of rock, more snow.

For von Igelfeld it was a curiously passive experience. This awful thing that was happening to him was, he realised, death. This was the end, and he felt curiously calm. It did not matter; there was nothing that could be done about it. And he thought: I failed to say thank you to the woman in the red jersey. She helped me so much and I did not thank her. But she will understand; I shall write her a letter and explain. No, I shall not be able to do that for I shall be dead. Well, my lawyer can write to her and say that Professor von Igelfeld would certainly have written to thank you for your kindness were it not for the fact of his untimely death. That was a consolation. And the second edition of *Portuguese Irregular Verbs*? The lawyer would contact the chairman of the Max-Planck Foundation and explain what had happened. He would understand too. Snow. More trees. He was travelling very fast now and there was a sharp pain in his side. This was most inconvenient. So very . . . He was airborne again, but the sky was dark and he could see nothing. Perhaps night had come. He saw a face. Herr Huber. And Herr Huber was looking at him in a way that presaged some remark about his aunt, but instead he said: *You have been so kind to me.*

Von Igelfeld was found not by the Librarian but by a passing mountain guide who was escorting two visiting Japanese climbers. The guide's heart gave a lurch when he saw the inert form spreadeagled in the snowdrift; he had witnessed a climbing accident a few months ago and the memory was still distressing; for it to happen to him again so soon was surely bad luck. But as he and

164

his clients approached the snowdrift, there was a sudden movement and then, to their astonishment and relief, the figure stood up and began to dust himself down.

It was obvious from the deep indentation in the snow that the fall had been from some height, but the guide was not prepared for the information that von Igelfeld, now quite conscious and suffering from no more than a bruised rib, proceeded to give him.

'It was very challenging,' he said. 'I was at the top of the Devil's Needles and I began a rapid descent. It was most uncomfortable, and potentially extremely dangerous for a less experienced person.'

The guide looked up at the towering, distant peak of the Needles. The Japanese climbers, who spoke no German, peered at von Igelfeld and exchanged quick, excited remarks intelligible only to themselves. The guide then looked back at von Igelfeld in disbelief. Perhaps this unusual-looking man was concussed; sufferers from concussion could talk the most extraordinary nonsense.

'Perhaps you were a bit lower when you fell,' the guide said politely. 'There's a ridge up there behind you. Perhaps you fell from there.'

'I know exactly where I was,' von Igelfeld replied. 'And I wouldn't necessarily say that I fell. I descended rapidly. There is a distinction, you know.'

The guide scratched his head and shrugged. 'If you

say so,' he said. He did not believe him, of course: no man could survive such a fall.

But it was then that the small radio that he was carrying crackled into life. A message had been transmitted from the party with whom von Igelfeld had been climbing and had been passed to the mountain rescue authorities. There had been a fall from the summit of the Devil's Needles and assistance was required in the search for what was assumed would be a body.

The guide listened to the message in frank astonishment.

'You see?' said von Igelfeld. 'That was about me.'

The guide nodded and let out a whistle of admiration. 'A miracle,' he said. 'A direct descent from the summit of the Needles. They said it couldn't be done.'

The Japanese climbers were now marvelling at von Igelfeld's height, rather than at the nature of the fall, the details of which, for linguistic reasons, they had missed. They now posed on either side of him, giving the guide a camera to record the meeting. Von Igelfeld tried to smile; he was a polite man – in his way – and would not wish to offend visitors to Germany, even when one of his ribs was most uncomfortable and he was now beginning to feel hungry.

He was escorted back to the lodge by the mountain

guide and the two Japanese climbers. More photographs were taken along the way and von Igelfeld also signed a small autograph album that one of the Japanese produced from his rucksack. By the time they arrived back at the lodge, the press was already there in the shape of the reporter from the local newspaper and a correspondent from *Mountain Gazette* who happened to be staying in the area.

Von Igelfeld was examined by a doctor who announced that his only injury – apart from a few scratches – was to a rib, and that would heal naturally, even if it would be uncomfortable for a few days. Von Igelfeld was stoical in these matters and did not think that painkillers would be necessary.

He agreed to speak to the press, but only later that day, once he had had the opportunity to catch up with correspondence and deal with some proofs that had arrived in that day's post. He did, however, meet his climbing companion, whose party had come down the mountain as quickly as possible – by the conventional route – after von Igelfeld's tumble.

'I am so delighted to find you alive,' she said. 'I never imagined that anybody could survive such a fall. When I saw you slip . . .'

Von Igelfeld shook his head. 'I'm not so sure that it was an actual slip,' he said.

'But—'

Von Igelfeld cut her short. 'No, I certainly left you abruptly, but an abrupt departure is not the same thing as an involuntary one.'

The mountaineeress stared at him. 'You are a very brave man, Professor von Igelfeld.'

Von Igelfeld gave a modest shrug. 'All of us are capable of rising to the occasion,' he pronounced.

'Or falling to it,' she muttered.

The reporter from the local newspaper realised that he had a major story on his hands. Sitting in the common room at the lodge, he sent off a piece that would appear the next day in all the major German papers as well as in a slew of foreign ones. *Celebrated Professor in Rapid Mountain Descent*, he wrote. *Professor Dr Dr Moritz-Maria von Igelfeld will go down in mountaineering history as the only man to make a descent of the famous Devil's Needles by the most direct route.*

The following day, when the papers were delivered to the lodge, von Igelfeld, still basking in the attention of all and sundry, waved a hand airily when the Librarian read out the phrase about going down in mountaineering history.

'I should have thought it better to go *up* in mountaineering history,' he said, 'rather than *down*.'

There was silence. Then all the students, the administrators, and Herr Huber began to laugh. Von Igelfeld bowed his head modestly, as a further

168

mountaineering reference came to his mind. What had Mallory said when asked why he had attempted to climb Everest? *Because it was there.* There were some amusing remarks, he thought, that had to be made – *because they were there!*

He looked about him. It was a relief to be alive, and in appreciative company. Herr Huber was looking at him proudly from the other side of the room and suddenly he remembered how he had seen the Librarian's face on his way down the mountainside. And what was it that he had said? *You have been so kind to me.*

He crossed the room and drew the Librarian aside. 'I appreciate what you have done here,' he said. 'You have made this reading party a particular success. Thank you so much for all you have done, Herr Huber.'

Herr Huber beamed with pleasure and made a noise that was difficult to interpret, but was clearly a noise of satisfaction, rather like the purring of a cat.

fünf

Unusual Uses for Olive Oil

The news of von Igelfeld's narrow escape from death was still being talked about in Regensburg a few days later, after the reading party returned from the mountains. The public reaction was generally favourable, with pride being expressed in the ability of the local professoriat to survive the apparently unsurvivable. People are, by and large, keen to find instances of human heroism, and the view soon emerged that surviving the fall was somehow an achievement akin to battling one's way down a mountain against extreme odds or reaching the South Pole single-handed. *This is a mountaineering triumph*, wrote one correspondent to the local paper. *In an age when even the climbing of mountains has become a high-tech business, here we have an enthusiastic amateur showing that what counts is determination and character. Professor von Igelfeld may be an unlikely hero, but he is certainly an authentic one. The city fathers should name a street after him – at the very least.*

This letter was read out loud in the coffee room by Herr Huber – in the absence of von Igelfeld – and the Librarian nodded in vigorous agreement when he came to the final sentence.

'There you are,' he said. 'I have often thought that it would be a good idea to have a street named after our dear colleague. I thought this even before this latest incident. I pointed out to my aunt . . .'

'Well really!' exclaimed Unterholzer. 'I have every admiration for Professor von Igelfeld, as we all know, but naming a street after him is ridiculous.'

'Why not?' asked Herr Huber. 'Professor von Igelfeld did a remarkable thing. It is quite appropriate to name a street after somebody who pulls off a major sporting achievement.'

Unterholzer snorted. 'A major sporting achievement? Come now, Herr Huber; what did Professor von Igelfeld actually do? He fell. Now I don't think that's a major sporting achievement at all. It's just a fall. And he turned out to be lucky enough to survive. That is not an achievement in my view. It is an outcome. That's all.'

The Librarian looked down into his coffee. 'I was

there,' he muttered. 'And I saw how high that mountain was.'

Unterholzer pursed his lips. 'Mountains are, by definition, high, Herr Huber. That is why only very experienced climbers should try to get to the top of them. Rank amateurs – professors and the like – should not venture beyond the very lowest slopes lest they stand the risk of falling – as a recent event has clearly demonstrated to us. And I fail to see what credit there is in falling – I really do. I could fall down the stairs outside my office any day, but I would not expect a street to be named after me as a result.'

'Well, he certainly managed to stay alive,' ventured Prinzel. 'And I, for one, would be happy to see a street named after Professor von Igelfeld.'

'Yes,' said the Librarian, emboldened by this show of support. 'And imagine how amusing it would be, Professor Prinzel, if you found yourself living on Von Igelfeld Street and he found himself on Prinzel Street! That would require, of course, that you do something heroic too, and I wouldn't want you to think that I would wish you to fall off anything. Perish the thought! I am sure there are many other reasons why a street should be named after you. For example, if . . .'

Unterholzer glared at the Librarian. 'Von Igelfeld Street?' he mocked. 'Let us remind ourselves what Professor von Igelfeld's name actually means:

hedgehog-field. People would drive down it very carefully because they might think that it was a street much favoured by hedgehogs. People do not like to drive over hedgehogs in their car. No, it would be very impractical.'

The suggestion that a street be named after von Igelfeld was taken no further, but the effect of the incident continued to be felt and von Igelfeld found that invitations to speak on the radio flooded in. There were several television appearances too, and requests for interviews from journalists. He tried to accept as many of these invitations as he could – not out of any personal vanity, but because he believed that it was in the Institute's interest to have exposure in the press and also because he believed that a measure of publicity would do no harm to the prospects of *Portuguese Irregular Verbs*. Von Igelfeld had always believed that his *magnum opus* should reach a wider readership, and it was a regular affront to him to be informed by the publishers that on average only two or three copies left their warehouse every six months. If further public mention could be made of it, then surely more copies would be bought and his work might perhaps nudge its way on to those lists of bestselling books he had seen in the papers. After all, there was no doubt but that many people were interested in language, and if even a small proportion of these were to read *Portuguese Irregular Verbs* it would make a difference.

In due course the interest in the mountain incident subsided. There was still the occasional invitation to make a public appearance, but the papers, having extracted all they could from the story, had other events to cover. What did arrive, though, was an approach from a speakers' bureau in Cologne, asking von Igelfeld whether he might consider becoming what the writer termed an 'inspirational speaker'.

He read the letter with some interest. *We represent a wide range of public figures*, it said. *These are figures from the business world, the world of politics, or, as in your case, the world of sporting achievement. There are many clubs and other organisations that are keen to engage such speakers for their meetings and dinners. Might we interest you in this? We have already received an enquiry from a business association in Hamburg asking us whether we can secure an engagement with you. Would that be possible?*

Von Igelfeld looked thoughtful. Hamburg was an interesting proposition, as that was where Zimmermann lived and if he went up there he could combine the speaking engagement with a call on Zimmermann. He and Zimmermann had a great deal to discuss and on the last two occasions he had visited Hamburg Zimmermann had been away. And it would be helpful if Zimmermann were to realise that he, von Igelfeld, had public speaking engagements. He could write to him and say, quite casually, that he happened to be coming to Hamburg to speak at a large dinner and would it be possible to call?

Von Igelfeld mentioned the letter in the coffee room that morning.

'A speakers' bureau?' said Prinzel. 'Interesting. I've read about such things. I heard of one retired politician who went on the speaking circuit and became a very wealthy man just speaking to people about things. An agreeable way to earn a living, if you ask me. And free dinners too!'

'It would be very nice for Professor von Igelfeld to do that too,' said the Librarian. 'I'm sure that there are many people – not just in Hamburg – who would like to hear him speak. I would certainly pay for a ticket, wouldn't you, Professor Prinzel?'

'I certainly would,' said Prinzel.

Unterholzer lowered the paper he was reading. 'I am sure that you would be very popular, Herr von Igelfeld,' he said. 'But what would you speak about, I wonder?'

Von Igelfeld shrugged. 'There are many things to speak about, Herr Unterholzer. But I might observe that the letter goes on to say something about an inspirational subject.'

'Your recent experiences in the mountains would be very interesting to people,' said Herr Huber. 'You could perhaps entitle your talk "Going Up and Coming Down". You could talk about how in life we are sometimes faced with circumstances that take us up, and then we encounter circumstances that bring us down. Up and down. That is how it is. And then you could tell them how to make sure that they go up more than they go down. And it would all be to do with your remarkable recent descent of the Devil's Needles, where you went up, and then came down.'

Unterholzer listened with increasing irritation. 'Or going sideways, perhaps?' he said sarcastically. 'There are plenty of people who might prefer to go sideways. What about them? How are we to inspire them?'

The Librarian, momentarily nonplussed, looked to von Igelfeld for help.

'It's all very well to mock at such things, Professor Unterholzer,' said von Igelfeld. 'All this talk of going sideways cannot obscure the essential truth that there are many people who do not know where they are going, whether it be up or down, or, indeed, sideways.'

'Backwards too,' said the Librarian. 'I imagine that there are many people who feel that they are going backwards. These are the people to whom we should reach out.'

'Nonsense,' snapped Unterholzer. 'Most people aren't going anywhere. And they certainly don't need inspirational speakers to tell them that. Not in my view, anyway.' He paused. 'Although I'm sure that Professor von Igelfeld would be a very entertaining and much appreciated after-dinner speaker.'

'Exactly,' said the Librarian. 'And do you think that you might perhaps come and speak at my aunt's nursing home, Professor von Igelfeld? There are plenty of people there who could do with a bit of inspiration.'

'I would be very happy to do that, Herr Huber,' said von Igelfeld, glancing reproachfully at Unterholzer. 'After all, we should all be willing to shoulder our broader responsibilities to the wider community.'

And at that point the discussion ended. Going back to his room, von Igelfeld looked again at the letter from the speakers' bureau and dictated a reply. He would be happy, he said, to accept the Hamburg invitation and he suggested that his talk might be called 'Going Up and Coming Down'. He hoped that the organisers would find this title acceptable, and he looked forward to the occasion in Hamburg.

I am delighted, wrote back the director of the bureau several days later. *I have already spoken to our clients and they are extremely pleased that you will be coming to speak to them. They are sure that their membership will be most interested in hearing you and they look forward to being your hosts in Hamburg.*

Now that the invitation was confirmed, von Igelfeld began to write his speech. He had a great deal to say on both going up and coming down. Going up, he pointed out, was a matter of commitment, preparation, and careful execution. Commitment required one to be determined to achieve the objective in question. *Do not be half-hearted,* he wrote. *Those who are half-hearted often only get halfway.* He stopped. The aphorism was neatly stated and utterly memorable. He was proud of it. And as for preparation, there could be no doubt but that this was the key to successful execution. *A prepared position is a position,* he wrote. *Those who are not prepared do not have positions. They may be keen to move into positions, but they are not there until they have made their preparations. When I go climbing, I always ensure that I have my ice-axe and my . . .'* He paused to think about what other pieces of equipment the well-prepared climber should have. *And my other pieces of necessary equipment,* he wrote. Again he was struck by the aptness of the advice and its elegant expression. Being an inspirational speaker, he decided, was not a difficult job at all – very much easier than being a professor of Romance linguistics, and rather better paid too, it seemed.

*   *   *

'Exciting news,' said Herr Huber that evening, as he sat in the small Italian restaurant that he had recently taken to frequenting.

His companion, Aalina, was the young woman he had met on the reading party.

The friendship that had blossomed in the mountains had survived the transition to lower altitudes – indeed it had become more intense. Now, sitting in a discreet corner of La Tavola Sienese, they held hands across the table, gazing at each other with an intensity of fondness that impressed itself even upon the waiters who had witnessed numerous romantic trysts.

'Oh, Stoffi,' enthused Aalina. 'I *love* exciting news. I love, love, *love* it!'

'Don't we all?' said the Librarian. 'It's about Professor von Igelfeld.'

Aalina's eyes widened. She stood in awe of von Igelfeld – an impossibly remote and grand figure if you were, as she was, a lowly postgraduate student. And now, to be in a position to hear first-hand gossip of his doings . . .

'Hamburg,' announced the Librarian. 'He's going to Hamburg to give a talk to a group of businessmen. This isn't a lecture: this is a talk. The sort of talk that prominent politicians or famous actors give. That sort of talk.'

Aalina absorbed this. 'You'd give lovely talks, Stoffi,' she said.

The Librarian laughed. 'Me?'

'Yes, you. You'd be really popular and there'd be big turnouts. Why don't you?'

Herr Huber shook his head. 'Impossible. Nobody would ask me.'

'I would.'

He pressed her hand. 'That's because you're kind. No, nobody would come to any talk I gave. Nobody wants to listen to me.'

She returned the pressure of his clasp. 'But I do! I love listening to you, Stoffi. You make me laugh. You make me feel . . . well, you make me feel as if anything could happen. You know that feeling?'

'Me? I do that?'

'Of course you do.' She paused. 'You know, I didn't tell you this when we were up in the mountains, but all my life – all thirty-whatever years of it – I've wanted to meet somebody just like you. A nice man. A good-looking, exciting man. Somebody who would make me feel . . . well, the way I feel when I'm with you.'

The Librarian said nothing. He looked down at the pattern of the tablecloth. Was he really a good-looking, exciting man? Would she say such things if she did not mean them? He thought not.

'You're so kind,' he said eventually. 'And I have also been looking for much the same thing, *mutatis mutandis*, of course. Now Fate has brought you to me.'

183

'And you to me.'

'Exactly.'

There was a silence.

'Yes?'

'Yes?'

Laughter. 'We must try not to speak at the same time,' he admonished. 'We must wait. I'm afraid that that is a lesson that Professor Dr Unterholzer needs to learn. He's always interrupting me when I'm telling a story.'

'Nasty man.'

'Not really nasty – it's just that he does not think very highly of me. Professor von Igelfeld is different, you know. He has always been good to me. He's a good man, you know. Not everyone realises what a good man he is.'

She nodded. 'They know about *Portuguese Irregular Verbs* and they're . . . they're blinded by his eminence. They don't ask themselves what sort of man lies behind the book. How kind and understanding he is.'

They were well-expressed sentiments, and Herr Huber entirely agreed with them. He entirely agreed with everything that Aalina said, in fact. He cleared his throat. 'Aalina?'

'Yes?'

'I hardly know how to put this, but I was wondering

whether it might be an idea for us to get married. I was just wondering.'

'That would be very nice. I would love it. Seriously *love* it.'

The waiter appeared with their first course and they were both silent while the plates were placed on the tables. Then, when he had gone, Herr Huber took her hand again and said, 'My aunt will be very pleased with this news. She has often said to me, you know, that I should get married. I remember her saying something to this effect only a couple of weeks ago, just before the reading party. One of the nurses in the nursing home had recently got married – to a man who came from Düsseldorf, I think. I believe the nurse was from Düsseldorf too, because of the way she spoke. You can always tell, you know . . .'

Von Igelfeld travelled to Hamburg by train and was met at the railway station by the secretary of the businessmen's association he was due to address. A room had been reserved for him at the Hotel Vier Jahrezeiten and he was taken there directly from the station.

'It is our finest hotel, Herr Professor,' said the secretary. 'And they have the Association's instructions to attend to any needs that you have. We shall have our dinner in one of their dining rooms. They have very fine chefs.'

Von Igelfeld nodded.

'And your talk, Herr Professor? How long will it take, do you think? This is just so that we can make arrangements for the dinner. And I must say the title is very intriguing. "Going Up and Coming Down". Very intriguing.'

'Thank you,' said von Igelfeld. 'Two hours. Perhaps slightly longer.'

The secretary froze. 'Two hours, did you say, Herr Professor?'

'Yes,' said von Igelfeld. 'It will be in four parts, you see. Two will deal with going up, one with coming down, and one will consist of a summary and conclusions.'

The secretary looked about him furtively. 'Is that not perhaps a little long, Herr Professor? This is a dinner, you see, and . . .'

'I do not think it at all long,' said von Igelfeld. 'It is very difficult to deal adequately with a topic in a shorter time, in my view.'

'But most of our speakers in the past have confined themselves to about twenty minutes,' said the secretary desperately. 'After a dinner our members tend to feel . . . somewhat replete. They are quite prepared to listen to longer addresses during the day, but in the evening, well . . . they are human.'

Von Igelfeld looked at the secretary with disapproval. 'Are you suggesting that I cut my talk? Is that what

186

you're suggesting? That I should perhaps just talk about going up and say nothing of coming down?'

The secretary looked miserable. 'I shall have to discuss this with the committee,' he said. 'But I fear that its view will be the same as mine: two hours is a very long after-dinner talk, I fear.'

They were standing in the hotel lobby. Von Igelfeld looked up at the ceiling in an attempt to master his irritation. 'This is most vexing,' he said. 'It truly is. But the last thing I should like to do is to cause any ill-feeling. And therefore I shall speak for no more than one hour.'

The secretary cleared his throat. 'I would never wish to appear difficult,' he said. 'But we were thinking more in terms of . . . fifteen minutes. I am sure, Herr Professor, that you can be admirably concise. It's a great art, don't you think? Conciseness. In the days of telegrams people knew all about it. Now, with all this e-mail and what-not, people have lost all sense of economy when it comes to words, don't you think?'

Von Igelfeld stared at the secretary. He would not answer this question, he decided. One did not have to answer all the questions put to one in life, particularly ones so otiose as this was, posed by one who had just deliberately *insulted* him by suggesting that a carefully prepared speech be *butchered*. He remained tight-lipped:

he would have no alternative but to teach these people a lesson.

The dinner began with a reception in one of the hotel's public rooms. Von Igelfeld, having been collected from his room by a nervous and now rather uncomfortable secretary, had been introduced to the chairman, Herr Lehmann-Wolf, and the five or six members of his committee. They had then taken him around to meet the members, of whom there seemed to be at least one hundred and fifty, all talking at the tops of their voices. He was warmly received.

'We are very honoured indeed,' said Herr Lehmann-Wolf. 'We pride ourselves on getting the very best speakers. And you are certainly in that category, Herr von Igelfeld. And something of a celebrity, too, after your mountaineering achievements.'

Von Igelfeld inclined his head. He was beginning to feel mollified, but he was still smarting at the discourtesy of having his prepared speech cut by such an amount. What could one say in fifteen minutes? Very little worth saying, in his view. But if that was the way they wanted it, then he would show them. They asked for brevity: they would get it.

There was a great deal of champagne. White-jacketed waiters, unctuous in the way in which the staff of all great hotels are, appeared at the elbow of every guest to ensure that no glass remained unfilled for long. Von Igelfeld, who drank very little, sipped modestly at his glass and resisted attempts to refill it. Such restraint was not evident in the broader membership, who became rowdier and rowdier as the reception continued. By the time Herr Lehmann-Wolf announced that the company should go through for dinner, the volume of noise was such that von Igelfeld could barely hear anything that was said to him. Was this the way businessmen behaved at their associations? Imagine if this sort of thing happened at philological congresses, sedate affairs at which champagne had never been offered as far as von Igelfeld could recall.

They sat down to dinner. The champagne was now replaced by white wine, which the same waiters, with the same persistence, poured into the members' glasses. This seemed to increase the volume of conversational noise, augmented by the sound of knives and forks on china.

'Our members rather enjoy these occasions,' said Herr Lehmann-Wolf. 'They perhaps rather let their hair down, you know. Hard work, I suppose, is often followed by hard play.'

Von Igelfeld nodded. 'Others work hard too,' he said.

Herr Lehmann-Wolf glanced at his guest with concern. 'Of course, of course. I wasn't suggesting . . .'

'They might work very hard on a speech, for

example,' went on von Igelfeld, 'only to discover that it is to be truncated.'

Herr Lehmann-Wolf did not hear this, as the remark coincided with his neighbour on the other side saying something about protective tariffs. 'Of course,' he said politely, to both. 'How interesting.'

The dinner continued. Over the dessert, an elaborate chocolate confection, Herr Lehmann-Wolf explained to von Igelfeld what his own firm did, which was to make guidance systems for small aircraft. Business was good, he said, as there seemed to be more and more small aircraft about.

'They are very noisy,' said von Igelfeld.

Then came coffee. By this point the membership was in a thoroughly good mood, and there had even been a suggestion from one table that there should be a sing-song. This was politely rejected by the chairman, who tapped on his glass with a spoon to restore order and to introduce the evening's speaker.

'Our speaker this evening requires no introduction,' he said. 'Not only is he a distinguished mountaineer, but he is the author of a book in Portuguese. He is very well known in Regensburg, and places like that. He is, of course, Professor Moritz-Maria von Igel, and I now call upon him to speak to us.'

This brought prolonged and enthusiastic applause, and even one or two hooting sounds from a table at the back of the room. Von Igelfeld stared down at the table. This was quite intolerable. A book in Portuguese! Places like that! And then, of course, the final insult: von Igel *simpliciter*. Professor Hedgehog. There was no excuse for such rudeness, even from a man whose name, when translated, meant Serf-Wolf. Hah! Not even a land-owning wolf, but a serf-wolf! He would show them.

He stood up. 'I am most grateful for this invitation,' he said, 'and for the opportunity to speak to such a distinguished group.'

Distinguished by their noisiness, he thought. Hah!

'I have been asked to be brief, and I believe that brevity is indeed a great virtue. The title of my talk is "Going Up and Coming Down". Now what does this mean? That which goes up, can go down. That is the meaning we can extract from the title. That which is long can become short. That which is brief, can become even briefer. So be careful in your dealings. Remember that those of you who are up – or high, in your case this evening – can also go down. Don't forget that. That is all I have to say.'

He sat down, tight-lipped. He had taught them a lesson; it had to be done. But then, no sooner had he resumed his seat than a wave of sound, of wild applause, surging like the currents of an incoming tide, reached him. The members were delighted. They clapped and clapped. Then they started to rise to their feet to give him a standing ovation. There were cheers ringing in the air.

'A very good speech indeed,' said Herr Lehmann-Wolf. 'As you can see, the members are quite delighted.'

Von Igelfeld did not know what to say. The secretary, who came up from the end of the table to congratulate him, said, 'I must say, Professor von Igelfeld, that you have charmed the membership with your speech tonight. You have very cleverly assessed our needs. So kind of you.'

Von Igelfeld nodded graciously. His hand was being seized by members seated nearby and, as he rose to leave, a further round of applause broke out.

'A triumph,' shouted one of the members.

'Brilliant,' called out another.

'They like you,' said Herr Lehmann-Wolf, smiling broadly. 'Ever thought of being a Hamburg businessman, *alter Schwede*?'

Von Igelfeld was too shocked to say anything. Herr Lehmann-Wolf had addressed him as *old Swede*, a very familiar mode of address indeed, and quite uncalled for in this context.

'No?' said Herr Lehmann-Wolf in answer to his own question. 'Oh, well . . .'

Herr Huber looked at von Igelfeld from behind his desk in the Institute's library. There was nobody else in the room, but the Librarian made it a rule to talk in a muted voice in the library, even if nobody else was there.

'Hamburg,' he whispered. 'How did it go?'

Von Igelfeld made a casual gesture with his hands. 'You know how they are up there. Very good hosts. Nice people.'

The Librarian nodded. 'I knew a man from Hamburg,' he said. 'He was a librarian too. We studied together . . .'

'Yes,' said von Igelfeld. 'Yes indeed.'

'And Professor Zimmermann?' asked the Librarian. 'Did you see him?'

Von Igelfeld shook his head. 'He was away,' he said. 'But he left a note for me saying that we should meet soon. Those were his words: meet soon.'

'Very satisfactory,' said Herr Huber. 'And they liked your talk? I knew they would. Will they invite you back, do you think?'

Von Igelfeld smiled. Poor, unworldly Herr Huber; he clearly did not know that guest speakers were usually invited only once. 'I don't think so,' he said. 'They have different speakers each year, you see.'

Herr Huber looked disappointed. 'Oh, well. There will be many other invitations stemming from this one, when word gets out.' He paused. 'And in fact one has already come in. Have you looked in your in-tray yet?'

Von Igelfeld had not. He was busy working on the

final draft of a piece for the *Zeitschrift* and had found no time so far for correspondence.

The Librarian explained. 'Professor Unterholzer and Frau Professor Unterholzer have invited everybody for dinner – as they did last year. That's you and Professor Prinzel and Frau Professor Prinzel and me and . . .' He hesitated, smiling shyly.

'Is there anybody else?' asked von Igelfeld.

'My fiancée,' whispered Herr Huber. 'She is invited as well. Specifically. By name. The future Frau Huber.'

It took von Igelfeld a few moments to absorb what had been said. 'Your *fiancée*, Herr Huber? *You* have a *fiancée*?'

Herr Huber beamed with pleasure. 'Yes,' he whispered. 'And you've met her . . .'

Again a few moments were required for von Igelfeld to order his thoughts. Then the memory came back of the sight of Herr Huber walking in the mountains with that young woman whose name he could not quite recall; of the comment that she sought out the Librarian's company. So that was it . . .

'I must congratulate you, Herr Huber,' he said. 'I never thought it possible . . .' He paused. No, he could not say what he was thinking. 'That is, I never thought it possible that you would find somebody who met your high standards. I am delighted that you have.'

Herr Huber accepted the compliment gravely. 'I have been very lucky,' he said.

'And she has been lucky too!' said von Igelfeld. 'She has been lucky to get you!'

'Do you really think so?' asked the Librarian.

Von Igelfeld wanted to say no, but could not. 'Of course I do,' he lied. 'You will both be very happy.'

'Well that's very kind, Herr von Igelfeld. And you'll all have the chance to get to know her better when we meet at Herr Unterholzer's house next week.'

Von Igelfeld looked down at his colleague's left hand. Yes, the Librarian was wearing a ring – a large gold band on which, even at this distance, could be made out an incised pair of entwined hearts. He glanced down at his own, discreet signet ring with its tiny hedgehog motif, drawn from the crest of the von Igelfeld family. He could never wear a ring with entwined hearts, but somehow, now, it seemed less lonely, less demanding than a single figure of a hedgehog rampant.

After his experience of arriving too early at the Prinzel house, von Igelfeld was careful to arrive somewhat later at the Unterholzers'. This meant he was last, everybody else having arrived at exactly the time stipulated by Frau Professor Unterholzer.

'Ah, there you are, Herr von Igelfeld,' said Unterholzer, adding, 'at last.'

Von Igelfeld looked at his watch. It was ten minutes after the appointed time.

'I have always believed that it is polite to arrive a few minutes after the time on an invitation,' he said. 'This gives one's hosts the opportunity to make last-minute preparations.'

'Not necessary in this household,' said Unterholzer. 'This meal has been ready since yesterday. And the table was laid two days before that.'

They went into the sitting room where the other guests were already seated. Herr Huber sprang to his feet and introduced Aalina. 'You've met my fiancée, of course,' he said proudly.

Von Igelfeld shook hands with Aalina and proceeded to greet Frau Unterholzer and the Prinzels.

'What a happy gathering,' said Prinzel. 'And how opportune it is to be able to wish every happiness to our newly engaged friends.'

'A very good development,' said Unterholzer. 'May you have many happy years together, Herr Huber and . . . and the future Frau Huber.'

Von Igelfeld raised the glass that had been pressed into his hands by Frau Unterholzer. He thought, even as he drank the toast, how bleak was the prospect of many years with Herr Huber. Could such years really be happy? How many hours of sheer boredom lay before the unfortunate Aalina – hours of tedium stretching out like the great German plain itself. And yet women were funny about that sort of thing. So many of them appeared to be perfectly satisfied with the most unlikely men, failing to see their manifest drawbacks, failing to object to their monotonous conversation, their wretched hobbies: fishing, motor-sport, beer – that sort of thing. Not that Herr Huber was interested in those pursuits; he was more focused on nursing homes and the issue of where people came from and how long they had lived there. Poor woman! Did she know that, he wondered. Was she aware of what she was doing?

'Herr Huber tells us that you had a very successful visit to Hamburg, Herr von Igelfeld,' said Prinzel. 'A standing ovation, no less!'

Unterholzer's eyes flashed. 'Sometimes people are very keen to get out,' he said. 'That may look like a standing ovation, but it is just getting up to go. Not that this was the case with Herr von Igelfeld. I'm sure that his standing ovation was quite genuine.'

'I'm sure it was,' said Ophelia Prinzel. 'Well done, Moritz-Maria! It will be London next. Then New York.'

Von Igelfeld smiled. 'I shall not be accepting any more such invitations,' he said. 'Like all of us, I have work to do here in Regensburg.'

'A very noble sentiment, I must say,' said Prinzel. 'There is nothing worse than these people who dash

197

about the place shamelessly giving talks. Have they nothing better to do?'

There were murmurs of agreement from all, and the next subject was broached. This was a discussion of road repairs near the Prinzels' house. Then they moved on to talk about Venice, and whether it was best to go there in the summer or the winter. Then there was something about a concert that Ophelia had attended recently where she was sure the piano was out of tune. 'The pianist looked most uncomfortable throughout the performance and at the end he banged the lid shut and swore. I heard him. I was in the front row.'

'That is quite inexcusable,' said Frau Unterholzer. 'It does not help to do such things.'

There was further agreement on this matter, and that took them to the point at which dinner was served. Over the meal, the conversation was congenial, with everybody making an effort to include Aalina in what was said. She proved to be an easy conversationalist, smiling charmingly at anybody who spoke to her and nodding agreement with everything that the host or hostess said. For the rest, she gazed upon Herr Huber with intense pride, not noticing, it appeared, that he told the same story twice, once at the beginning of the meal and once towards the end. This was a story of a man who came from Bonn but moved to Frankfurt, and then went back to Bonn.

Halfway through the meal, von Igelfeld spilled a small amount of gravy on the cuff of his shirt. Attempts to remove the stain with his table napkin having failed, he asked permission to use the tap in the bathroom for this purpose. 'I know exactly where it is,' he said. 'Please continue for a few minutes without me.'

He went out into the long, book-lined corridor that led to the bathroom at the back of the house. Halfway down this corridor, sitting strategically on the carpet, was the Unterholzers' dachshund, the unfortunate Walter, with his three-wheeled prosthetic appliance strapped round his sausage-like stomach. On seeing von Igelfeld approach, Walter rose to his remaining foot and attempted to wheel himself out of the way. He was not fast enough, and von Igelfeld, who was not looking where he was placing his feet, tripped over him.

The dog gave a yelp and attempted to move further out of the way. Unfortunately this was not possible, as von Igelfeld's foot had kicked off one of the dog's wheels. Now unbalanced, the dachshund simply fell on his chest, letting out a whimper as he did so.

Von Igelfeld looked down at the dog at his feet, its little wheel clearly detached, lying beside him. Bending down, von Igelfeld picked up the wheel and, calming the dog as best he could, attempted to fit it back on the appliance. It was very stiff, and he had to give it a good push before it found its place, but this had the effect of driving all the breath out of the dog, who had to gasp for air.

The wheel in place, von Igelfeld gave the dog a further push, to see whether all was working correctly. It was not. The wheel that he had replaced now refused to go round at all, so that the dog turned in little circles as he paddled with his remaining leg.

Von Igelfeld had no difficulty in arriving at a diagnosis: the wheel needed oiling. But how to do that?

The dog, in the interim, had moved in circles through the kitchen door, and it was in the kitchen that the solution presented itself. Reaching up to the shelf above the sink, von Igelfeld took down a bottle of extra virgin olive oil and dripped a small quantity over the bearings of the non-functioning wheel. Then he tried to ease the wheel by spinning it. Unfortunately he forgot that he was holding an open bottle of olive oil in his other hand, and as he leaned forward he tipped the contents of this bottle all over Walter and the surrounding parts of the kitchen floor.

Walter, alarmed by being covered with olive oil, let out a howl of protest and ran – in so far as a dog with a prosthetic appliance and three wheels can run – back along the corridor and into the dining room, to seek the succour of his owners.

Von Igelfeld put the now empty bottle of olive oil

back on the shelf, made an unsuccessful attempt to mop up the spillage on the floor, and returned to the dining room. The conversation was still in full swing, although Frau Unterholzer was looking down in puzzlement at the floor beside her chair where Walter, covered in olive oil, was licking at his coat. She glanced up at von Igelfeld and frowned, but he avoided her gaze.

At the end of the meal, Professor Unterholzer left the table to turn on the coffee-making machine in the kitchen. A moment or two after his departure, there was a loud thud from the kitchen. Frau Unterholzer gasped and hurried from the room, to return a few moments later with her husband, who looked flustered and uncomfortable. They both glared at von Igelfeld.

'My husband slipped,' said Frau Unterholzer. 'But he is uninjured.'

'I'm so sorry to hear that,' said Herr Huber. 'At my aunt's nursing home they have these special non-slip floors. You can't slip on them – it's just impossible.'

'If one covered them with olive oil, one might,' said Frau Unterholzer darkly.

'Possibly,' said Herr Huber. 'But why would one do a thing like that?'

The Prinzels had come by car, and they gave von Igelfeld a lift back to his apartment. As they drove through the night, Prinzel said, 'A very pleasant evening, don't you think, Herr von Igelfeld?'

Von Igelfeld looked out of the window; a city looked so different by night; indifferent too. 'Yes,' he said. 'Very pleasant.'

Ophelia Prinzel turned to look at von Igelfeld in the rear seat. She was fond of him – and always had been. Poor Moritz-Maria: all alone with nobody to go home to. And there appeared to be oil stains all over the front of his shirt and on the sleeves of his jacket. How strange.

'Are you happy, Moritz-Maria?' she asked suddenly. She did not know why she asked this; it just seemed to be the question that needed to be asked at the time.

'Happy?' he asked. 'Why should I be anything but happy?'

She shrugged. 'I don't know,' she said. 'It's just that the world sometimes seems a bit unkind, doesn't it? It can be unkind to people who just want to be loved, like everybody else; who just want that – no more, just that.'

'Well, it's not been unkind to me,' said von Igelfeld.

He looked out of the window again, at the passing world – a world of night and loneliness. A world in which there was a place for some but not for all. Did he believe the words that he had just uttered – that the world had not been unkind to him? He tried to believe what he said – he tried – and that, perhaps, sometimes enables us to believe what we wish to be true.

'Yes,' he muttered, half to Frau Prinzel and half to himself. 'I have much to be thankful for, as most of us do.'

'That's true,' she said, reaching out over the back of the seat to place a comforting hand upon his forearm. She felt the olive oil on the fabric of his sleeve, but did not worry about that, because sympathy – and friendship – can rise above, can negate, the misfortunes that so consistently and so unfairly beset others. Sympathy and friendship can rise above these things – and almost always do.